Sean Ennis

Hope and Wild Panic

Hope and Wild Things is a work of fiction. It is copyright ©2024 Sean Ennis. Quotes for review, scholarly, or other purposes that fall within the realm of fair use are welcome. All rights belong to the author.

The cover was designed by Angelo Maneage. Find more of his work at angelomaneagethewebsite.com.

ISBN: 979-8-9903240-0-8

Published August 2024 by Malarkey Books.

This book is set in Mala, a font designed in 2016 by Barbara Bigosińska.

For Claire:

Big Things

Table of Contents

Acquiring The Muse	11
Irenic	12
Nuptial	14
Honeymoon Reverie	16
Source And Scale	18
The Flora Of Water Valley	20
Vorarephobia	22
Crowded Afterlife	24
Airbnb (St. Louis)	25
If I Am A Fool	28
Brazen	29
Family Incantations	31
Robust And Infrequent	32
Dream So Bad	34
Hope And Wild Panic	35
The Convalescent	57
Something Is Knocking	58
The Goof, Meredith	60
Expectorant	62
The Fauna Of Water Valley	64
The Ambit Of Our Friendship	66
Professionalism	68
Expertise	70
Lake Enid Idyll	73
The Three Types Of Despair	74
On Turning Forty-One	75

ACCOUNTING	77
UNABASHED	79
AS A NEW RULE, I DON'T MISS THINGS	81
ME, THE KINK	83
BACK AGAIN	85
THE OUIJA ALONE	88
WITCHES OF WATER VALLEY	90
JEALOUSY	92
DEEP PLAY	95
AIRBNB (CHATTANOOGA)	97
WHEN ANIMALS TOUR THE ZOO	99
SEX LIFE	101
THAT VASECTOMY TALK	103
HEART OF A MOCKINGBIRD	105
NOT HERE BUT NOW	107
THE HOME, A DESERT	109
THE POLITICS OF WATER VALLEY	111
AURAL, GESTURAL, SPATIAL	113
MY WIFE'S PHONE	115
INFAMOUS	116
KIND, HEATED HOUSE	118
O NAMES IN THE GRASS	120
PLEASE NOBODY	121
AIRBNB (MOBILE)	124
LEARN FOR HER	125
JUSTICE	126
FERVENT WAITING	128
WOOD STREET IDYLL	130
THE CANNIBALS OF WATER VALLEY	132
JEWELER'S ROW	133
CLEAN, SLICE, INFLATE	135
DISAGREE AND COMMIT	137
FOR GRACE AFTER 9 P.M.	139
WE DON'T ENCOURAGE STOPPING BY	1141

SWAMP FOX	143
A FEATURE OR A BUG	145
AIRBNB (BIRMINGHAM)	148
I'M UP! I'M UP!	151
BORED, THERE WAS A RAINBOW	152
I HAD A CHAUVINISTIC THOUGHT	154
I'LL SAY THIS THEN I'LL SHUT UP	156
HER HEALTH WAS GENERALLY FINE	158
GRACE'S MELANCHOLY	159
WOE IS GRACE	161
GRACE COMES OUT OF IT	163
VOUCHSAFE	164
GRACE IS FOXY	166
FOXY BUT WRONG	167
WOMEN LESSONS	168
THIS IS WHAT WE TRAINED FOR, PEOPLE	171
WES'S BETRAYAL	172
TIMOROUS	173
THAT ASPECT OF HAPPINESS	175
YALOBUSHA COUNTY IDYLL	177
THE FUTURE IS NOT URGENT	179
PROSTRATE	181
CLOSING THE BOARD	182
SEVEN YEARS	183
COMMISERATION	184
GNASHING	186
DEAR AGGRIEVED FRIENDS	188

Acquiring the Muse

How great to be working on a biography. Now I'm acquiring a muse. Sometimes, a poet says, "My heart is like" something-something. I'll try.

My heart is like an air fryer.

My heart is like a Super Soaker, a super-spreader.

"I'm just grateful to be here this morning" is definitely AA speak.

Irenic

Sad! Grace's first husband died when he lost control of his car. A hornet had gotten in. She obviously survived—seat belts, people!—as did the bee. She believes herself to be the only woman widowed in such a silly way. As a child, I was stung on the face at an apple orchard, and my limited knowledge of melittology informs me that I am now immune. Thus, our romance.

Today, we've planned a lunch date and then we're going to buy some quasi-legal drugs. We're looking to giggle. I have never been married before but came close-ish. I'm also going to experiment with different settings on the dishwasher, for Grace.

When there's a full moon, like tonight, Grace leaves a jug of water and a plate of special stones on the deck to charge up in its light. I have very few opinions about this practice. I let it proceed as if she asked my permission.

The woman I almost married still thrives presumably. But, lo and behold, my memories of her are evaporating. I recall she had IBS and intense freckles on her shoulders, but I can't conjure up her face. Is this an effect of Grace and her magic rocks? Again, I'm okay with it.

She was widowed at twenty-four, and I met her on the steps of a university building while she was near completion of her program in grief. I invited her to a party I was throwing and she didn't accept. What happened instead: I gave an idiot a whole bottle of scotch to just leave my apartment. Love was not ready.

Grace wears black all the time and, oh no, it occurs to me now she may still be in mourning. I don't think highly of this guy or appreciate him. He was in my way and may still be.

Can you imagine? A bee!

We also have tickets to *Angels in America* performed by puppets tonight.

When I stop to reflect on why we have such a busy day planned, oh god no, it's the anniversary of the accident. I don't even want to look at a calendar.

What little I know about the deceased. People, take your lives seriously because they might end up a joke.

Nuptial

We just wanted to screw in a nice hotel. We're going to be married, maybe order room service. The pandemic has been good to us—we got vaccinated early because we smoke. That's the calculus of our luck. But also, what would we do with the dogs and our son while we lounged suite-wise?

The new roof, you'll want to know, has held through the winter, though it snowed in Mississippi and the temperature dropped below twenty. It is a comfort. Spring now and baseball is back and the fans from Arkansas have booked all the hotel rooms. Like I care.

But *I do*. Our team is highly ranked and her friends are throwing a marriage party. The match should be exciting. The trick here is that I am talking about both sports and a wedding. Did you catch it? There will be no bouquet because we are not that type.

I found her—convincing her was easy—I believe somewhere that I am lovable. But the lawyers have taken all the hotel rooms and I had thought for a minute about becoming a lawyer. I have thought, too, long and hard, about becoming a husband. There is no test, but a thousand tests.

I can't say enough about this little family, almost outnumbered by dogs, and clinging. Achieved in reverse. The rings will arrive in the mail. She found me—dying to know—she brought me here.

Still mad at those alumni lawyers, their whole floor of rooms, their diminution of us—nice try! We say *big things,* mean it, then get ready to go to Sonic.

But a young woman has stopped her car in front of the house. She's crying. How sorrowful to just leave the engine running.

Finally, I approach the car saying, "Please do this somewhere else. We're going to be married soon. My fiancée is literally on roller skates." Grace was practicing.

"No one cares," she says, which could mean, "I don't care," or it could mean, probably more likely, more accurately, more in tune with the general state of things, upcoming wedding aside, "Hectoring pitilessness."

She wipes her nose and drives off around the corner. When we get to Sonic, I order something bright blue, potentially cancerous, and delicious.

Honeymoon Reverie

I really thought the Sonic was burning down again, but it was just one car with white smoke spewing from its tailpipe. The descriptor here is "engulfed." A cop pulled the driver over when he pulled out, but didn't arrest him or beat him—they popped the hood and looked in together. From my vantage, it was all relatively good news for me. I was watching from the Piggly Wiggly parking lot, just rapt with how all this action might play out.

Then a shopper dropped two dozen eggs in the parking lot. She started to cry. My day was going better than literally everyone I had encountered so far. As a sightseer, I was providential. This was the good life.

Now, in the store, they are selling pink Himalayan salt! Chili-infused honey! The rewards program got me $2.37 off! Was that a fresh jackfruit? It's ugly, enormous. I bought one.

I got married two weeks ago. Every single woman and man in the Piggly Wiggly wanted me, but they cannot have me. The only reason I'll take off this ring is if I have to work on some small motor, which I have never done before. An accident would shred the hand.

Can I believe someone loves me? Can the myth of divorce rates be true?

When I got home, my bride was gone. A tomcat has carried off two of her friend's new kittens, and they are out listening in the vacant lot for them. To find them would be a victory, but also a crisis in the local cat ecology. When our own cat was finally fixed, it was filled with kittens.

So true that what pleases upsets some. That guy, who I mentioned, with the car, the smoke? I know him, in another manner, to be a neighborhood creep, but I was rooting for him. I was. My bride's exes? I hope they neither moved on, nor ever show up.

Source and Scale

In my study of love, I once attended a graduation. All the students, they implied, had been blessed with a job. The guest speaker said, "In effort there is joy." Kabul fell during the ceremony.

I like to watch Grace try on new clothes, even the junk from Old Navy. Sometimes she says the word "panties" or inadvertently touches her breast. I say, "Yowza." She'll return half of it—she's no fool. Grace narrates a bit while I wince on the bed. She moves the black T-shirt, the black tank top, and the black pants to the pile to be kept. "Cute," she says.

Oh Lord, don't send me back.

Doubling down on it, I close the horny door, but the show is over, and Grace is back at war with her computer. The semester starts in a week. We both have desecrated our adult lives to the intellectual well-being of young people, mostly between the ages of seventeen and twenty-five. We know a ton of other people who have done this too. This is just one of the reasons why I don't now hold a powerful position in city politics. There are others. I'm not a liar anymore. Etc.

Our sheriff has passed, and there's a line of cop cars, even the hastily painted undercover, delivering his body to the funeral home. We can see the blue lights from the bedroom window, and we get saddish for a second, though, as they say, we voted for the other guy. That bad criminal, pneumonia, has won.

I already get embarrassed when the trash truck comes, though we innovate by recycling. The neighbors have gotten new gravel for their driveway—I pity them—which is not interesting or gossip-worthy, but they keep pulling in and out to smooth it. Do they enjoy their work? He is a graduate student and she is a graduate student and at night they play the worst music with their little girl. Have they never heard of, like, The Beatles or Rimsky-Korsakov?

But at that very moment, not a single other person on Earth was thinking about me. Not even this woman asking me questions. Where do you see yourself in five years? Right, it was an odd question. I have always been victim to the thought, if two is good, four must be better. Some have given it up because it is too violent; others because it is not enough.

This was not a date or a job interview, but we were practicing. It was just Grace making conversation. There's a trust one must have when completing jigsaw puzzles, and this is what we had. I stopped watching the news right after they reported that plants can see and feel pain.

The Flora of Water Valley

This itinerant tree surgeon says, a thousand dollars, after cutting at one of our trees and lifting it off the ruined fence.

For a tree? I say. Was it made of diamond?

Five hundred, he says.

Put it back, I say. Here's some super glue.

Two hundred.

That's perfect. It's not like I was going to chain myself to it—it was a weak and cowardly tree. And so we come to an agreement: let's lug these logs to the street like real business partners.

Now the fence. The dogs can smell freedom from inside and I can taste freedom so I get some twine and rig it up myself, tree money having jeopardized fence money.

I called the man a tree surgeon, though I'm not sure that's a real job or how he identifies beyond Robert. I guess my sad intent was to disparage his hustle, which is strong and lucrative, two hundred dollars. You can tell by the debris at the curbs that the trees in this town don't want to stand up anymore, and Robert has the tools. There's this effluent whiff of wood. He said he's been tending to our trees longer than we've owned them. I had been impressed, but it faded pretty quick in the humidity. As much as I keep talking about him, I'd rather move on.

Because my biggest fear when my son's friends sleep over is that there'll be a home invasion. My own friend calls to tell me about his daughter who is now a karate black belt. If only my son hung out with lethal kids like that, I'd have a lot less to worry about. Whatever, I've felt like an imposter but there are also those times when I feel as though I'm just secretly on to something. What would make me feel safer, filling out gun paperwork? Three, no, now just two angry dogs? Still, I always end the interview when someone asks can you protect what's yours. There's that reptilian feeling one gets while watching fireworks.

Robert, here I go again, was back the next night, running his saw through the rain at the neighbors'. What crisis was he inviting, what accident attempting?

Now he is waving. We are not friends.

Now I'm on a group text with Robert and the candidate running for coroner. How many doors does your house have? What happens to your loved ones when you die? When *they* die? What about that other tree?

That one is a cedar that smells not so much like freedom but more like that time you threw away the map while walking in the woods. It's too tall to hear shaking in the wind. If it were to fall, it would split this green brick house like a melon, we breathe its air at our own peril. Still, I'll defer that disaster, tree money having jeopardized other tree money. Though it looms.

Vorarephobia

Fear of being eaten is an evolutionary relic, but sometimes I do feel the twinge when I see a cement mixer, or a jet engine, or a customer service representative from Verizon.

"I want to talk about something which is interesting only to me," I say.

The chimpanzees on the television show had a good day. They successfully defended the northern border and when they got back, there's a marmot infestation. Marmot meat is delicious. It's a beautiful afternoon in Uganda, and yes, it's fucking fig season. But all is not well—the chimp, Worthington, has been brutally murdered!

The question is, did we unfairly overlay a human narrative, or do we really find close representations of ourselves in these animals? I mean, this is a really fascinating question. If you were really interested, you could do more research if you weren't too busy.

It's Mother's Day, so Grace is sleeping in while Gabe and I prepare her favorite breakfast. I assume one of the reasons Gabe prefers his mother to me is that he's known her nine months longer.

People can talk their way out of things. They can make symbolic gestures to avoid being devoured. I've done research, and shopped for and prepared the ingredients. I present my inconvenience as a part of the gift. The real difficulty, of course, is that I'm chasing after a memory that Grace has of this dish, and, again, the minds of others are a mystery.

Now the chimpanzees on the show are getting hungry again. They're starving. They're chewing on these leaves you can tell they don't even like. A friend requests we meet somewhere private to talk. I suppose he has the right to do this—I assume the worst. "What have you heard?" he said.

"Basically nothing," I said. "Nothing true, probably."

We were talking in a space so public, it was private. Everyone was ignoring everything. It was the correct behavior in a grocery store parking lot.

My friend starts in on his, "What will happen? Where will I go?" when a cashier rushed outside, yelling, "You left your card!" at another customer.

"I have no use for it," the woman said. She was crying and had no groceries.

"It's going to be okay," the cashier yelled back.

Money eats again, and here, it is not fig season. When the episode ended, the chimpanzees were mourning for Worthington. But when the credits roll, in the dark forest, do the chimps eat their friend? They *are* ravenous.

CROWDED AFTERLIFE

Two guys from the Sober Living house on Highway 9 were outside the Piggly Wiggly asking for donations. I had been to a couple AA meetings there and felt usually that I might be killed off by one of the other attendees. Lots of wood paneling, ankle bracelets, violent Jesus talk, and dirty dishes. No women or even a feminine touch. Of course, we're all on our own journey. I didn't donate, though they almost called out to me by name.

I have reached my free limit with Grace—must now pay and subscribe. So we watch a documentary about a haunted house a few counties away. The argument seems to be that if there is enough limestone in the ground below, souls spend the afterlife in the house, putting forth the excruciating effort to open doors and push baseballs down the stairs. I don't agree with this night-vision argument. My only insight about the afterlife is that it must be filled with so many insects, so many you can't even go outside.

Airbnb (St. Louis)

Under what circumstances do we find ourselves here? The house is a duplex, the top half like staying inside a skeleton, the furniture simmered down to stock. There are no towels and the silverware is kept in a jar on the counter. The coffee maker is definitely a fire hazard. This part of the story is about staying in someone else's home so we don't know the cat that has taken up on the porch.

Right, this is St. Louis, everybody, and those were screams last night, right? Something went knock-knock on the, what, the TV, the back of the couch? The dominant impression is that the previous owners were surely murdered, but they still send email, arranged our stay on the app. There is a presidential-type portrait of a llama and I swear its eyes follow you from the bedroom to the toilet. But the door at the bottom of the stairs locks itself so we are safe, trapped. What else happens in haunted houses? It could probably happen here too.

Breakfast is hip and then we visit the botanical gardens, which are resplendent, I mean, redundant and filled with cosmos, I mean, cosplayers. It's the Japanese Festival so there's a sumo match amongst the bonsais and it's so hot we're dripping with culture. Here's your twenty-first-century balloon animal, a stressed-out octopus. Here's mine: just dread in balloon shape.

Back on our second floor, maybe just the skull of the house, we take a breather. Weird sunset glow. The llama in the shadows minding its business. The walls are bloodless.

My wife takes a nap before dinner. Sometimes when I think she's gone from me forever, she'll reach out and just touch my stomach. If there were some other villain, she wouldn't do that. I check the weather and surmise my own garden at home is dying in the heat. The carpenter bees probably sawing up the deck. Our dogs: holding it.

Where is the Arch, that gaping mouth? I want to see down its throat to a startup in California. But there is this cloud ceiling and pouring rain on the interstate. We'll get there Sunday. In order to build suspense, I tell my son the Arch is so old it was probably built by aliens, how else could it be done? But no, he googles it instead, childhood magic searched away. "It sways," he says. "Eighteen inches."

Still, the storm, so the City Museum instead, a church in praise of American junk and tunnels. I'm not describing it right, but a kid is stuck in a tube many stories high and another is bleeding in the school bus suspended off the roof. Do you understand the place now? It smells like a lawsuit inside or like the inside of a helmet. Friends said it was a must-see. Our kid gets lost, found, says, "Boy, was I worried."

One of the purposes of a trip like this is to see the country. Another purpose is to bring the family closer together. My wife orders squid ink pasta, and I think, *I love this woman.* Under a placard announcing Yogi Berra's birthplace, my son says, "Who the fuck is Yogi Berra?" He should watch his language, but I love him too. But what have I done that's lovable? Carried the luggage from the car into the spooky duplex? Killed the spider that had built a web across its door?

An old injury in my ankle is acting up, a surgery, all this walking. I have money problems. The job is a drag. Thirteen kids killed in this city this summer. This house is no hotel. On our last night, I can hear my heart in my ears.

Now the screaming Arch with the sun at its peak, the metal pill it swallows to get to the top and its small window. As a family, we decide panic is not worth the view. Mississippi the River, poet-killer, is blue-brown. The museum underneath is a grave for cowboys and Indians, and the gift shop is mobbed, so we're headed back to Mississippi the State, which is green-brown. I've said the duplex locks itself.

Did we accomplish our purposes? We actually saw no ghosts as a family, and there is some regret. Speaking of haunted, I read somewhere that the deaf wonder if the sun makes noise, and are also disappointed.

If I Am a Fool

I was watching the Impeachment when the dog walked through the room and it occurred to me that golden retrievers are supposed to be nice. That dogs understand and appreciate they've been rescued is not always true. That dogs like to be petted is not always a good plan of attack. Take this one for instance.

I mainly need to know if I am a fool. My son doesn't even ask for help with his school project and what do I know about Indonesia anyway?

I mean, the dog was probably abused, his stomach was full of rocks when he showed up. But you still don't, like, tie a bandana around his neck and throw a Frisbee.

This is the worst part of the day, walking to this appointment across the parking lot by the stadium and the bell tower. He won't want to meet or be friendly or even acknowledge actual feelings. He'll bring a lunch, the reason he's late. Sometimes it's hard not to see my whole big picture in this encounter.

Be optimistic! There are plans in place. Next subject.

The dog sometimes requests attention (but then growls). My son needs something from the oven (after he burned himself). At this appointment I mentioned, I get up, I spin around, I stand on my head. Nothing works. A clown, like when your favorite team loses and you're still wearing their jersey.

Brazen

Gabe uses our bedroom like a hallway and then swears to his video game that someone is going to die. He doesn't notice his mother, who looks at me, is home already. The dog is exhausted from its own obsessions on the corner of the bed.

Grace says, "Is that really play?"

So I knock on my son's door with my usual *hey bud, what's up, take it down a notch*. He is still staring at the screen saying over gunfire, "I'm savage, you little bitch. Get got."

Now my Grace is saying, "Is he talking to me?"

The other dog, the one that is dying, that is deaf and blind, that seems to live fueled only by appetite, walks through the bedroom, pissing, and then falls down.

"C'mon," I say. "Let's go watch the eclipse."

"Oh, more hell," my son says.

"Take a picture," my wife says.

Outside, the moon is burgundy. Just a rim of it glows white. I think, *I must stop whatever this is*. It's brazen. I don't want to be dead, what with the beautiful universe clicking into place, a loving wife, a healthy child, but I'd like to be finished. I can't tell if the eclipse is starting or ending and I have no access to those feelings right now that might be moved or awed.

Back inside, the dog that is not dying is off the bed and fussing again about the corner by the bathroom in the hallway. He paws at it like he's seen a ghost. Something must be dead behind that wall. It's all the dog cares about. The rest of us are just keeping him from it.

Gabe comes back into our bedroom. "Top three!" he says. "It's a calamity that I lost."

"Are you using that word correctly?" Grace says. She's removing nail polish. The dog's pee is cleaned up. She got some towels.

"It's almost bedtime," I say. "You have piano in the morning."

"What is this? The Army?" Gabe says. We were off to a terrific start with him, but now.

"You could benefit from a real, short battle," my wife says.

The dog that is dying is facing our bedroom mirror, looking dumb. The dog that is not dying has to have its anal glands expressed tomorrow anyway.

The lights go out in my son's room, though Grace and I both know he keeps playing his game. We don't say anything to each other about it. If we did, it would ruin us.

"How was the eclipse?" she says.

"When did I get fat?" I say. "It must have happened recently."

I sit down at my own computer. Someone has mistakenly become my friend and is experiencing and documenting what seems to be a complete mental break. I cannot bring myself to like his posts or to end the friendship.

For instance, he posts, "There's a lunar eclipse and it's making me rage."

He posts, "My boss, that bastardess."

He posts, "Stop calling for wellness checks, I'm fine."

I fear I hold his life in the balance. He has collected witnesses for something. This whole thing is like being in the audience for a children's orchestra: cannot laugh or leave.

FAMILY INCANTATIONS

Ah, sweet escitalopram, tender aripiprazole. You're back, thanks to telehealth, and so is some order and peace. No side effects. I can story-tell with some logic.

We're under tornado watch and eating leftovers, so the family is ranking the best meals we've ever eaten. Certainly, Jiko in Disney World. That crawfish boil for Neal's thirtieth birthday. That chef's tasting at Tarasque for Grace's fortieth. Chickie's and Pete's after a long flight to Philadelphia for Christmas. That place in Breckenridge whose name we can't remember. We've done it all!

We also rank the worst meals, but I won't shame anyone here. I haven't been to that lawyer bar in five years, but I can imagine everyone there smug as health insurance, discussing racism and microplastics in our seas and our whales. I miss it only like I miss that good student loan money, which of course comes due with what they hysterically call "interest." What now?

Gabe reveals he's spied on me using the Ouija board and wants to play. I tell him first off, it's not play, and Grace says abso-fucking-lutely not. My sense is Gabe would bring a lot of good, productive, optimistic, youthful energy, so I betray Grace, and tell myself that my son and I will use it next time she goes to Colleen's.

The weather has not turned significant yet, and the pills are really gliding through me. The impulse to replay bad memories is almost gone. I wink at Gabe since it seems he only enjoys the past too.

Robust and Infrequent

Another Friday, another night spent admiring thousand-dollar quilts made by friends at the art gallery. I have absolutely no idea how they were made, unlike my big heavy book. They are truly shocking when thinking about quilt expectations. Take what you think about a quilt and turn it inside out. You don't sleep under them—they are more vertical.

Coincidentally, I am dressed in exactly the same clothes as the gallery owner (jeans, light blue button-down, shoes) and a customer asks me to tell the artist's life story. I say she must have grown up in a very cold household to be so inspired. Then he opens a wallet full of cash.

On the drive home, there is nothing said about the quilts because they were so fine and unobjectionable, not because we aren't artsy. Instead, Grace and I return to the movie we watched the night before. In it, the psychiatrist on the spaceship deems the whole crew unfit for duty, including himself. It's year five of a ten-year mission. Then the Earth blows up because of some vague scientific reason. Point being, the astronauts are all crazy, but now without any context. We agree the rest of the movie was trash, but, damn, if the beginning didn't give us something to think about.

For instance, our young neighbors have just erected a small, white picket fence in their front yard. That way, their toddler and their dog can play. But the rumor in town is that they are headed for divorce. You can watch their cars and tell. They also always miss trash day. It's like everyone knows but them.

So one of the first things I look at in the mornings is the "Love and Sex" page on *The Guardian* website to make sure Grace hasn't written a letter to their advice column. They are anonymous, but I'd recognize her diction and syntax. There's this one: "I love my husband—but his sexual limitations are blighting our marriage." Probably not Grace. The em dash seems off and I never heard her use any version of the word "blight." Then there's this sad sap: "I am not attractive to others. Would life be better if I made more effort?" That wasn't me—I wear cologne.

My "limitations" sexually? I *am* left-handed. I am incredibly nearsighted, so much so that an ophthalmologist once marveled that I must possess something equivalent to tunnel vision. I once tore my Achilles tendon coaching Gabe's soccer team, which still aches when it rains. Other than that, I think of myself as open to suggestions and willing to improve. No, no, it's not just "lights-out-missionary," as my father says, in that department. We are, Grace and I, I'd say, robust, if somewhat infrequent.

Dream So Bad

I had a dream so bad I couldn't tell Grace about it and Grace was in it! That my mind could concoct—that it would make me believe—I mean, I worry. My father tells Gabe a story about hiding in the woods from soldiers when he was a boy and eventually escaping to the freedom of Water Valley. It is a lie, of course. My father has lived in Philadelphia his whole life, and there is no history to hang this tale on. Still, what was once a story of adventure for a child has become a strange, political joke that Dad insists on at holidays. Our family was never refugees in this specific sense! There is the belief that someone played drums in the Civil War, but I haven't swabbed my cheek and gotten that confirmed. Okay, in the dream, I was being shown how to do something new, being talked into it, something I had never done. There was, like, an instruction manual and some encouragement. Let's just say if I did this thing, in real life, I would not just be weird, but monstrous. So twisted, so vile. Have you seen this trick? Ricky once filled an empty vodka bottle with water and took massive swigs at a stranger's party. People thought he might die, haha. "Are you Sally Ullman's former supervisor?" I am not. "Can you provide a reference?" She apparently has difficulty with email contacts, but my generalized and optimistic faith in humankind tells me she should be hired.

Hope and Wild Panic

1.

Before I quit drinking, something terrifying happened to us.

The restaurant was so crowded, what with the community trying to show its resiliency after the bombing the week before, that Grace and I shared a table in the barroom with another young couple. We figured these types of inconveniences were a small price to pay in order to stand up to senseless violence and terror. There was enough friendliness and suspicion in the air to inspire conversation.

We learned that Peter was a sculptor and Jill was a video artist who filmed him sculpting. But sometimes, they explained, he sculpted her filming things, and then a friend of theirs would design a website for the entire project. Fascinating, right?

We didn't understand art, but they dressed in ways that suggested they made a lot of money. For instance, Peter wore a necklace, and Jill wore polished military-style boots. And they had taken an interest *in us*.

All four of us ordered grilled oysters, garlic bread, and beer. We laughed. We community members, diverse as we were, had a lot in common.

Jill pointed to her breath and said, "No making out tonight!"

"Mints all around!" Grace said.

Peter and I laughed like old friends, as if to say *Can you believe these two? They never change.* Then there was a shout outside the restaurant—a woman yelling, "No!"—and the whole restaurant froze.

2.

Peter and Jill invited us back to their apartment for a drink. The scream of "No!" had been into a cell phone and seemed to be about some private problem that was resolved with a laugh. Nothing exploded. Grace and I looked at each other and shrugged. It was only ten o'clock; their apartment was within walking distance.

We walked away from our own place. Grace and Jill paired off and sped ahead. Peter took the opportunity to ask what *I* did. I explained that I helped student athletes navigate the rules of NCAA regulations and eligibility at the university. I made sure they went to class, didn't take gifts, and limited their social media presence.

"I've always hated jocks," Peter said. "It's an easier stance to take when you're a teenager. But they are still out there. Jock adults. Don't you agree?"

"I don't know," I said. "These kids work hard."

"At games," Peter said. "What classes are they actually taking?"

"You know," I said. "Biology. Comp. Algebra."

"Blech," Peter said. "Not art and philosophy, I bet. Bullies." It was starting to seem that Peter was fueled by something more than a few beers. "Tell them you know an artist with a very sexy wife," he said. "Grace too. She's gorgeous."

Up ahead, Jill and Grace were giggling, their foreheads almost touching. They seemed to be connecting in a way that Peter and I were not. Still, I found myself defending my student athletes, if only in my mind. It was true that most saw me as some sort of administrative water boy, that quite a few of them would be earning more money than I could ever imagine in just a few years. But it was also true that many of them would tear or break something vital and find themselves selling used cars. Or worse. Some would rattle their brains so badly that they couldn't recognize themselves in a mirror.

"Are we almost there?" I said, and then watched Jill and Grace drop down and out of sight.

3.

Theirs was a basement apartment. It was pitch dark inside, except for the purple neon light in a tropical fish tank, and Peter and Jill made no move to illuminate the place.

"We have bourbon, scotch, gin, rum, vodka, tequila . . . ," Peter said, and we could hear a cabinet open and the clink of glasses.

"Some decent wine too," Jill said. "White, red, or pink?"

Music began to play. It was some kind of free jazz tumult, a piece you might write an essay about but shouldn't share with new friends over cocktails.

A new light source emerged, the bulb in the freezer.

"Oh crap," Peter said. "Our ice maker is shit. I'll be right back. Make yourselves at home."

Jill whispered to Peter before he left, and then turned to us.

"If you like your drinks neat, by all means fix one," she said. "But if you'll excuse me, I have Crohn's disease and must use the bathroom."

4.

Alone in the dark apartment, Grace and I huddled by the light of the fish tank.

"I love these two," she said. "They are so *interesting*."

I tried a few of the light switches on the wall, but nothing happened. On closer inspection, there were no bulbs in the fixtures.

"What's the deal?" I said.

"I don't know," Grace said. "It's like old-timey. Imagine what they save."

The electric bill in our household was always a bitter fight. I left the gigantic television on all night, long after I had fallen asleep. She was constantly bouncing the thermostat from arctic to tropical.

"Peter seems like an angry guy," I said. "He went off when I told him where I worked."

"Jill said she and Peter were out that night of the bombings," Grace said. "They saw some crazy things. Help me find a corkscrew."

"Is that what you two were giggling about?" I said, but she had already walked out of the light cast by the fish tank toward the kitchen. I heard a drawer open and the clank of metal.

"Ouch," she said. "That's not it."

When I found her in the dark, her hands were rifling through a drawer full of knives. She held one up that had a serrated blade and a forked point, and she poked me with it.

5.

Peter returned with two bags of ice and a brown paper bag. "Here we go," he said. "Where's Jill?'

"She said, 'Crohn's,'" I said.

"Ah. Shitting during the party," he said. "It means she likes you."

Peter slammed a bag of ice on the kitchen floor and then tore the other bag open on the counter like some sort of melting cornucopia.

"There we go," he said.

An animal we hadn't known was there darted toward the ice that fell on the floor.

"That's Cigarettes," Peter said. "He's a pig. You don't eat swine, do you?" The pig was grunting and chomping. "Everyone always says, 'Everything's better with bacon.' Give me a break. Is a sunset better with bacon? Is art better with bacon? Are bombs? Your jocks don't eat bacon, do they?"

Half of my student athletes outweighed me by a hundred and fifty pounds. I had no idea what they didn't eat. The other half had bodies as hard and pristine as gems.

The toilet flushed, then flushed again, and Jill came into the kitchen.

"Hello again," she said. "Thank you. Sorry."

6.

It's hard to make friends as an adult. Everything is work, kids, or sex. Everything is drinking, politics, or home improvements. Maybe pets. Maybe something medical. Standing in their dark kitchen, I vowed I'd call my best friend from grade school, a guy I deeply admired and loved, and whom I dreamed about more than I actually talked to.

Peter put four glasses on the counter next to the bag of ice. "What will it be?"

I thought again of my best friend, years ago at a college party, filling an empty handle of vodka with water and strutting around, taking monstrous gulps to shock the drunken crowd. I was at his side, saying, "He'll do it! He's a beast! Just dare him!"

"You know," Jill said, and Peter pulled a square bottle of tequila into the light.

"Sure," Grace said. "Me too."

This was not my wife's typical choice. She was being polite but also signaling that she cared little about the consequences at the moment. She was indulging in a rare moment of fun. Tequila was a drink whose chemistry made her flirty, then philosophical, then angry. There was empirical proof. Three or four of those and she would be sick in the morning.

Peter pointed to me.

"I'll have what you're having," I said. I vowed I would drink only from the same bottle and at the same rate as our host. Peter smiled, acknowledging the age-old pissing contest that is drinking among men. If the women were drinking straight tequila, we'd have to raise the stakes pretty high.

"Perfect," Peter said. He reached into the darkness and produced a cut-crystal decanter. "Try this."

Grace and Jill resumed their private giggling. What Peter poured tasted like gin, but I would not be the first to speak about it. I just swallowed and nodded.

"You're wondering about the lights," Peter said.

"Sure," I said. "It's pretty dark in here."

"There was a fire," Peter said. "An electrical fire."

"A huge fire," Jill yelled from the living room.

"It was a little scary," Peter said. "Our landlord is on it. But it will be a few days."

"Crazy," I said. "Scary."

"It inspired us a little," Peter said. "What is art without light?"

"Great question," I said, though I thought only crazy people would tolerate this. When the heat was broken in our apartment, we spent a few nights with Grace's folks.

"It's fucking death, right?" Peter said. "It's profound."

"Is the place not up to code or something?" I said.

"Ha! Code!" Peter said. "That's your thing, right? Follow the code? I'm going to call you 'Hammurabi.'"

"I just meant the wiring," I said. "I'm not an electrician."

"Come look at this," Peter said, and passed farther into the apartment's darkness.

7.

His beard was worth noting here. It was longer than one could attribute to laziness. It was clean and deliberate but extended three inches below his chin. Its rigidity suggested a certain amount of maintenance and petroleum. A very disciplined bird could have lived there.

But the corner on his left jaw was unbalanced. It was shorter and curled at its edges. Something in its hygiene was screwy.

8.

Peter turned on a flashlight in this new room. On the far wall, extending from the electrical outlet, was a burned-out fan reaching toward the ceiling. There had been a fire. It smelled of something cheap and ruined. The floor was stained too.

"It's all fucked up," Peter said.

The room was empty otherwise, no furniture, nothing on the walls. There were blankets covering the windows that faced the street.

"This was our workshop," Peter said. "Where the magic happened."

"How terrible," I said. "Were you guys hurt?"

"Not our spirits," Peter said, and scratched at the ruined part of his beard. "We press on, as they say."

We walked back to the kitchen, and Peter rattled the ice in his glass. We got refills and joined Grace and Jill in the dark living room.

9.

The women had lit a few candles, and the music had changed.

Grace pointed up. "Isn't this wild? It's the pope!" She was right. Pope John Paul II was reading prayers in Latin over what sounded like a Depeche Mode instrumental. It was really dumb.

"Cool, right?" Peter said. "How humiliating to the Holy Father." He laughed.

I was not a person of faith, but I wished for anything else to fill the room. Frank Sinatra, Run-DMC, Woody Guthrie, Justin Bieber. I also wondered what was powering the stereo.

Jill continued a conversation she and Grace had been having before Peter and I came back.

"I've tried everything. I eat nothing. I've considered infecting myself with hookworm, but they're tougher to get your hands on than you might think."

"It's a parasite," Peter said. "It has beneficial outcomes for digestion."

I nodded. That cleared things up. The oysters and the beer and whatever Peter and I were drinking started to sour my stomach.

"That's partly why we're going to East Africa next month," Grace said. "You can walk around barefoot and get hookworm. For free."

"Also, inspiration," Peter said. "I think we've sucked this place dry of it."

"I wish we could see some of your work," Grace said. She had taken an art history class in college and had been deeply affected by it. She could tell a Matisse from a Degas and a Monet pretty well.

"But the lights, right?" I said. "Maybe next time."

Peter looked at Jill and shrugged.

"I can show you what I'm working on now," he said. "But it's not done."

"How cool," Grace said. "Please."

10.

Peter went farther back into the darkness of the apartment, and Jill focused her attention on me.

"Grace was telling me about one of your poor students," she said. "Dorian?"

Dorian Williams was the football team's left tackle. I saw him as one of those villain's henchmen from cartoons whose brute strength was useful and intimidating but whose mind was simple and kind. He had recently been accused of sexual assault, and my office was trying to figure out what to do about it. He was six-eight, weighed three hundred and twenty-five pounds, and had an IQ of eighty. One might argue that any physical interactions he had with a person were a sort of assault. Football would either make him a very wealthy hero or destroy him.

"I can't say much about it, since there is an ongoing investigation," I said. "And he's not really my student."

"Every time I've met him," Grace said, "I just want to give him a hug."

"I bet a boy that big gives *great* hugs," Jill said, and the women laughed.

Dorian Williams probably was a rapist. He may have even been using the perception that he was simple and kind as a smoke screen for very bad behavior. It was unclear what to do with him. His backup was an underweight freshman, and the team was one win away from a pretty good bowl game. The athletic department where I worked was not a court of law, so we did everything we could to support him during this difficult time.

"He's a talented kid," I said. "I hope it works out for him."

"I'd like to video him," Jill said. "Raw power and hurt."

11.

Peter returned holding something that looked like a car battery. When he put it down on the coffee table, it sounded very heavy.

"Again," Peter said, "it's not done."

In the candlelight, the object seemed to be painted in rainbow colors, with a number of wires and terminals jutting out at all angles.

"Wow," Grace said. "What's it called?"

Peter smirked and looked at Jill. She smiled too.

"Who needs a drink?"

Grace stood up and swayed. "Count me in."

12.

It was clear to me then that Peter and Jill were the bombers from a week before. The darkened apartment, the fire in the workroom, and now this object, which, even with my limited sense of what art might be, could only be an explosive. Surely pieces like this did not sell for thousands of dollars in galleries and fund their fancy necklaces and boots and beards and liquor cabinet. We were being recruited into a devious plot, having mistaken their strangeness for coolness.

Or maybe not recruits. Victims made drunk and then beheaded. No, first reading some script while Jill films, then killed. Or strapped with some artistic bomb of Peter's and pushed out the door of this underground den of terror. I needed a plan.

13.

When they returned to the living room, Jill took Grace's seat next to me and handed me another drink. My mind was racing, and I thought the best thing to do was to drink quickly, not be suspicious, and call it an early night. Redirect the conversation whenever possible, away from that stupid work of art and politics and bullies and whatever else they were mad about and wanted us to be mad about too. If we had to get rid of whatever poison they were serving us with an emergency room visit, then so be it.

"I've heard some athletes are celibate all season," Jill said. "Saving their energy or whatever. Is that true?"

"I'm not a physical trainer," I said.

"Or an athlete," Grace said.

Last summer, our department and a few of the teams attended an award ceremony in Atlanta. Their seasons were over, and their accomplishments were being honored. The scene at the hotel pool was like Babylon. The girls' volleyball team strutted around in their university-issued bikinis, their long, tanned legs suggesting they played on some beach instead of in a gymnasium. The football team got rowdy in the water, displaying ridges of muscle only an anatomy teacher could identify. As I did some paperwork under an umbrella, the sexual tension was thick enough to choke on. The possibility that these young men and women were saving themselves for anything but each other was laughable.

I finished my drink and yawned. "Well, it's getting to be about that time," I said.

"Oh yeah?" Grace said.

Peter and Jill grimaced at each other.

I stood up and touched Grace's elbow. "We should get going," I said reluctantly, as if there were some babysitter waiting to be paid or a sad dog whining by our front door. In fact, there were no real obligations we were neglecting. Nothing calling us home but sanity and safety.

"Fine," Grace said. "You're right." She looked at her wrist as if to check the time, but she hadn't worn a watch in years.

"Oh, boo," Jill said. "One more drink. There's something else we want to show you."

"Thanks again for your hospitality," I said. "This was fun."

Peter was sulking now, taking our glasses to the kitchen, running them under the faucet. "Next time," he said.

14.

Grace and I walked to the nearest corner and looked at the street signs. We were lost.

"Peter had a vasectomy," Grace said, oblivious to our location. "Do you believe that? He's only twenty-seven." She was swaying a little and holding on to my elbow.

"Jill said he insisted," Grace said. "I guess it was meant to be a plus."

"A plus?" I said.

"I mean, I'm flattered, I guess," Grace said. "But it's just too weird. Right?"

"What do you think was going on back there?" I said. It was clear we were understanding our evening very differently.

"A foursome!" she said. "Or swapping or whatever! Oh my god!"

It hadn't occurred to me that they wanted sex. This would require more paranoia. But first we had to pick a direction. I gave Grace a shove north.

15.

The neighborhood was dark and empty now, but we had walked only five minutes from the restaurant. A few stragglers were muttering and whooping, and I figured if we walked toward where they were coming from, we'd find someplace familiar.

I didn't share my interpretation of the evening. The thought of Jill and Peter nude by candlelight dominated my thoughts. Peter's beard on Grace's neck. Jill looking meaningfully into my own eyes. Sure, they were an attractive couple, but the revulsion I felt was not about that.

We used to be dangerous and sexy. I'm not talking about the mile-high club, but still, we held our own. Now when Grace undresses for the night, I look at her and think, *Boy, I should really invest in a better lens cleaner for my glasses.* I think, *What's that dog out there barking about now?* Grace asks if it's cold enough to pull out my winter pajamas. Once, I threatened her boss, who was getting too touchy-feely at a Christmas party. The fucking bully. Once, before a beach vacation, Grace had gotten a Brazilian wax at the salon, and that sort of planning thrilled me.

16.

Back at our own strange apartment, the lights still worked. Grace stood in the doorway, crying because her feet hurt from walking, and then because no one had asked her about her own job, and then finally because we were friendless midlife-crisis clichés.

"You think Jill is sexy," she said.

"I think she's a weirdo," I said.

"You think Peter likes me," she said.

"Of course he does," I said. "But I like you more."

"Yeah, yeah," Grace said.

She turned on the harsh fluorescent light in the bathroom, and she was pale and sweaty. She picked up her toothbrush and pointed it at me. "I'd kill," she said, "for what they have."

17.

There were no more bomb threats, in our city at least. And there were no exhibitions by Jill and Peter at the local art galleries. I checked, unsure what I wanted to find out. If they were showing work, then I was just paranoid and still knew nothing about art. Their absence could mean any number of things.

It seemed Grace forgot all that she said to me that night. In the morning, she mumbled, "God, no more oysters for me." Whatever that evening had been, it wasn't what we'd thought.

The Convalescent

Gabe has been hit by a car! He's okay! He bruised his spleen! More details to come.

What I want to report on first is that this morning the message on the whiteboard in the kitchen said *Look Out!* I would have said something regardless of Gabe's incident.

The accident was at very slow speed and purely accidental. We live at the top of a hill and many lost drivers choose to turn around in our driveway. What they don't expect is Gabe chasing his basketball. Crash! Screams! The consecution of procedures here is familiar and dull once we know the outcome. Two days observed in the hospital, a tender belly. A dented hood, frazzled nerves.

But, rejoice with me, I have beaten anxiety. There's this trick I made up where I use the windshield wipers of my mind when it creeps in. Blood pressure is low except when it's checked.

And, oh Gabe, one of his virtues is bravery, hunched over and cursing, but we let him. The driver is an elderly woman who calls every night. She gives off the impression that she is guilty about more abstract things in her life and now wants to pay Gabe's hospital bills, which are not extensive and already covered. She has dropped off, carefully, a board game he has no interest in.

No doubt, the accident has disrupted my reflections and I have not forgotten the message on the whiteboard. That investigation is ongoing.

SOMETHING IS KNOCKING

Everything *bothers*. Everything *irritates*. I am not afforded the pleasure of anger.

So, bear with the setup here, please. Grace and Gabe, after saying something very cutting—Grace, not Gabe—have gone to visit her parents and I am home with the dogs, in the shower, flooded with the memory of a woman I once slept with who kept demanding, "Look at me! Look at me!" It's not, like, eudaemonic.

Then the dogs are going crazy. Something is knocking. They get very protective of the house when I'm in the shower. I don't hurry.

And let's be real clear: the dogs we rescued from the shelter? Did not rescue us. We do the nice, expensive things, and they basically hang out with their small, furry demands.

And let's be clearer still: what Grace said about the seance I hosted being "poorly attended"? I was not alone.

I decided to wear the Yves Saint Laurent La Nuit de l'Homme. Recently, I've been favoring the John Varvatos Vintage, but the Saint Laurent is Grace's favorite and I miss her. Her friend Colleen once told me, "You don't talk much, but you always smell good."

It's Meredith at the door, the woman who tried to kill Gabe. That's not fair. The accident was three weeks ago, and he has stopped complaining about his bruised spleen. The hood of her car is still dented, and she is holding a plate of cinnamon rolls, my favorite. She says, "I knew you were home."

In the living room, I'm rethinking her. She has the familiar, submissive demeanor of someone trying to get off drugs. The logo of her jeans is outlined in rhinestone, and good god, they are bootcut. She sits inexplicably in the chair possessed by Grace's dead grandmother.

"Did your family leave you?" she says.

"Permanently? No," I say. "Or rather, none of your business."

"You have pretty eyes," she says. "Are they real?"

Notice, she does not apologize.

THE GOOF, MEREDITH

Meredith, the woman who hit Gabe with her car, is still in the living room, sitting in the chair possessed by the spirit of Grace's dead grandmother. She'll be having visions shortly. Got it?

The stated purpose of her visit is to "check in." She is not now part of the family, despite the fact that she brought cinnamon rolls.

"What is your *real* purpose?" I say. "Gabe's spleen is healing just fine."

I had been prepared for meanness in this world, but not butt-kissing. It struck me as a low form of aggression.

But now the ghost of the chair has her, and she is most likely experiencing rural Georgia in the 1950s. She was killing chickens on a farm and being courted by a young man with Dax in his hair. She is being tortured by nostalgic Americana.

When the ghost releases her, she starts crying, which is the typical outcome.

"It's not like we're going to sue you," I say. "This is totally unnecessary, if not inappropriate."

"I keep running into your son in dreams," she says, standing now. "I need relief ... these cinnamon rolls."

Grace and Gabe are not home. I'm on my own with the whole ushering-her-out-of-here business.

As a child, I was run down on the beach by a golden retriever off its leash, and I'll never forget the way my father threatened the owner. No doubt, the dog was playing, but that breed bites more people than pit bulls. It's an actual fact. Things are getting muddled here, but what I mean to say is that our dogs are just waiting behind the bedroom door to get rowdy. Please don't mistake my kindness for enthusiasm.

Expectorant

More biography: I'm recalling the flowers of my youth, the perennial blooming of bronchitis in my young, sunken chest. Freezing cold and embarrassed by the X-ray machine, the young nurse: "You poor thing!" Filled with yellow, shadowy and gross.

But this is about getting Meredith out of the house. I let her in and don't know what to do with her. As Grace would say, "Well, this is a metaphor, isn't it?"

Robitussin with codeine had been too much for me and made me so nauseous I had to lay down in the back seat. Erythromycin gave me allergies. I had to go to second-tier treatment. I missed a whole basketball season but got a trophy. Some people think it's gestures like that that are ruining this country.

Meredith is still talking: "You know, you're the ghost that's haunting this house."

"I forgive you for hitting my son with your car, but not for bullshit, know-nothing statements."

She begs to see the dogs, and when I let them out, they all sit down in her presence. They were meant to expedite her exit, and this is unprecedented.

"The pups!" she says, which is wrong, wrong, wrong since all but one are full-grown.

I pick up my keys. "I have errands."

"And I'm blocking the driveway," she says. "I get it. I know your type. You leave blank answers on a multiple-choice test."

She drives off and I drive off to complete the lie. I have no such errands.

How dare she come into my house with her NA spiritualism. I know she's an addict because I'm an addict. It's not like I still have that trophy from the basketball season I missed with bronchitis. But what she said is not nearly superficial enough to be true.

The Fauna of Water Valley

Some people in this town complain that the church bells violate the noise ordinance. Some wash their cars at night so they're ready for the morning. Some think that showering during a thunderstorm could get you electrocuted. When it rains, the deer are out in the street. When the plumber changes the faucet in the kitchen, he says, "You don't drink this stuff, do you?" Some people say, "Well, you've been there long enough, it must be home."

The gentleman from the Electric Department says while trimming tree branches that my son is too athletic not to play baseball. Actually, he yells this from a bucket, thirty feet up, like some extracurricular god. My son hates baseball like a communist but has been to many games. He has a girlfriend now.

Sometimes I see the kid who stole my bike riding it around. He has spray-painted it gold. I hadn't ridden in fifteen years, but the loss bugs me. I want to tell him to go ahead and keep the bike, but know, you little jerk, that it looks pretty dumb painted that way. Maybe he can't afford a bike, but I still don't like the idea of him creeping around in my carport. And has he thought about how much a solid gold bike would weigh? Next time could he just ask?

Like the two kids who knocked on my door selling rakes— no, they wanted me to give them money to clear our leaves. The recurring suggestion here seems to be that I can't take care of my shit. They are appalled when I tell them no. What do I look like, someone who carries cash? Someone who keeps free bikes in his carport? Stop your lawn inspections, you tiny deputies.

Speaking of law enforcement, there's no smoking in the Piggly Wiggly. No pets. No green beans, but sometimes cactus, sometimes tofu. Many brands of energy drinks. No scallops, but alligator. A bake sale in the parking lot, a table selling homemade crucifixes. The clerks wear the earbuds. We can at least say the shoppers are vaccinated.

Our neighbors have a pig for a pet and the stupidity of this choice is fantastic, their refusal to eat it. After all, there's the palliation of the Sonic drive-thru, and overpriced ice cream at the gas station. No doubt, the pig smells the barbeque pit on Main Street—pigs are said to be smart. It's always wagging its tail, though I'd have to look up whether it's the same as a happy dog.

More headlines. A life-size painting of a deceased street preacher on a piece of plywood: also stolen. A jade-colored statue of a centaur in front of the Dollar General: defaced. The Redbox won't read your card. The good mechanic retired. The garden has those worms that look just like plants that eat your plants.

Now it's the show about animals on local talk radio and my son calls in to ask how you tell a boy-wasp from a girl-wasp. They give him the fucking runaround, they don't know. But what kind of strange boy hates baseball and ponders the sex of insects? I mean, I'm pleased when he tells me his girlfriend has dumped him, but not when he won't say more. Even his grandparents suggest we go to the *casino* to swim in its *pool*. What am I doing wrong? I don't know how to undo this.

THE AMBIT OF OUR FRIENDSHIP

I've been *accused* of having no ideology, but I've got plenty! And sometimes I just go with the algorithm. I like thinking that something knows what the heck is going on.

And I must be doing better. My old psychologist texted to talk shit about my favorite football team.

I say, *Hey, I'm not drinking, still, at all.*

He says, *Your team really was trash this season.*

I say, *You told me once it would take three years to get my shit fully together and you were right.*

He says, *Your guys better draft well or you'll be trash again next year.*

This is talk therapy, something I was encouraged to pursue, and do enjoy.

Wes is one of fifteen student athletes I've been tasked to tutor this semester. He comes from a town so small there is no exit for it on the highway. He is my favorite and also the way I'll be speaking about the entire experience of my job. I cannot say what sport he plays due to NCAA regulations but will give clues. Like, here's one: his goal is to score touchdowns.

From what I can tell, his class is a Möbius strip of writing assignments, each presuming to justify the last. His need, outside of this class, to master APA formatting is negligible.

Instead of working on his research paper about the dangers of space debris (my idea), Wes calls up his college recruiting highlight reel on YouTube. It has about two thousand views and there's some nice one-hand catches.

"You're the man," I say. "Now back to space junk."

"Wait," he says, and types my name into the search bar.

I predate the site, but somehow there's a video of Grace telling me she's pregnant with Gabe. There's me giving a complicated martini order to a teenage waitress at Noodle Bowl. Me butchering a skinned rabbit in our kitchen for stew. Me waking up from surgery with a joke already prepared for the nurse. Me failing to change a flat on a Louisiana overpass. Me signing up for Twitter. Me skipping metaphysics class so I could get a Ghostface Killah autograph. Me loading the dishwasher, me loading the dishwasher, me loading the dishwasher.

In the months we've been working together, Wes has probably put on twenty pounds of muscle. It *appears*, slowly but surely. Unlike his research paper, which is just blinking back at us at a dismal three hundred words.

Don't you see it? You don't get it?

Now I've brightened my phone and cleaned my metaphorical fish tank. I redirect and incentivize. I'm committed to truth and depth.

Was it cruel of Wes to reduce my life to clips on YouTube? We are not friends. He learns the Japanese are making wooden satellites to combat the problem of his essay. He's almost in tears looking at a map of what's all orbiting Mother Earth. He mourns for a minute the potential end of space travel. He's getting it. The work expands.

And of course that shocking footage was not on the site. It was a fantasy. It's just a little bit of what I think about when I think about me.

Professionalism

On the other hand, Grace did something wonderful at work. She shined a light in the dropped darkness. She saved an entire life! To say more might embarrass or betray or violate laws, but she did do it, nonetheless, was even given cookies for her actions. She drove all the way to where she was needed, and then went farther and further. I'm so proud of her.

Scene 2: I was on my kickback, thinking to myself, babe, chill, I'm on your side. But when do I reveal my tattoos to my new boss? What will I sing at work karaoke? This is all that's bothering me and living stress-free. I used to have such dread on Sundays at about 4 p.m.

I am searching for the sentence to say, I fucking know about lying in bed hoping the phone doesn't boing. I've felt no—solicitude. I was in the concussion protocol of the soul. I'm trying.

To demonstrate the difference between equality and equity you can use this cartoon of a ladder, but Jessica said, "What about justice?" then collapsed, puking. She had stopped taking her meds, then took them again, and now here she was. We were in the Great Hall with skylights—natural light—and then she ended up at the local clinic, then the city hospital.

I won't go so far as to say I saved her life—I mainly gave advice and directions. I didn't answer her question, but the answer *is* on another slide, a cartoon ladder with steel supports.

Scene 4: We kissed and Grace said she tasted blood. I know it's my undiagnosed gingivitis. Dental insurance is out of the question and can you imagine spending green money on your teeth? It's the twenty-first century and they still have at you with the metal hooks and picks and drills. I'm holding out for some good innovation.

Where is this going? By which I mean my professional life, by which I mean this local train. You come to a complete stop at the junction, then wait for the faster ones to pass.

Expertise

The way some people—including me—believe in their own expertise is distressing. I am not remarkable, I mean, marketable. So I tiptoe in and check on my money like a sleeping baby. I've been trying to erase the context of my past for five years. Do nothing with irony.

My schedule has not been formed yet, and I don't want to waste the dog's time, so Grace and I decide to go to the Golden Nugget in Tunica while Gabe is at school. It's either there or Home Depot and Applebee's.

On the drive, we plan our plan. I explain the three rules I know about craps. Grace shares that her mother once played penny slots in Atlantic City for ten hours straight and broke even. Remember, it is possible to place so many bets in roulette that you can't possibly win.

I will not judge the Wednesday morning crowd because I'm among it. First, I order a club soda and have to explain how the drink is made without vodka. Grace gets champagne with a pale pink raspberry lolling in it.

In the bathroom mirror, as prep, it occurs to me that something very dramatic, either good or bad, could happen today.

When I find Grace, she is faking her way through a hand of baccarat. There is a dude with a sapphire earring and a widow's peak perched on her shoulder, making suggestions.

There was a time when I would have made a big deal about this, but I've given up on petty jealousies. As newly expected, he glances at my tungsten wedding band and evaporates.

In college, a friend leapt over the wall on the top floor of a casino parking garage. He caught himself—this was not a suicide—but he had lost $5,000 of his student loan playing blackjack. He was a young man fueled only by bravado, bourbon, and quotes attributed to Ben Franklin. He had no intention of finishing art school. I loved him.

Then Gabe texts both of us: *we on lockdown*.

I hate to say we knew this day would come. Let's say, not so forcefully, not so I-told-you-so, that we are not surprised. We are, however, surprised to find ourselves ninety miles away at a casino when it did. As parents, we can honestly give ourselves a B+ cumulative rating, but this is D work that we've turned in today.

The official text from the school has now come in, confirming, and we're already aiming south on I-55 with $80 in Golden Nugget chips. I will not add to the general bemoaning about the modern necessity of enhanced school safety. If all Gabe learns in eighth grade is how to keep himself alive, plus a little algebra, so be it.

By the time we get to Batesville, Gabe has texted again: *lockdown ovah dude dropped a gun*. We are relieved by the profound mystery of this message.

When the official text from the school comes in, it seems the school resource officer misplaced his firearm. It was dutifully turned in by, get this, a third grader. We are happy, but I also swear to write an angry letter about this.

We had no chance at the casino—Grace didn't even learn to play baccarat or enjoy the effects of her dismal flute. On TV, there is a lot of hugging after school incidents like this, so we assume that will be our impulse when we see Gabe. He texts again: *what's for dinner?*

A week later, my letter to the editor is published in the newspaper. I write about the responsibilities that come with certain rights. I take a few jabs, but I'm not as angry as I thought.

Lake Enid Idyll

I'm here, live, from the shores of glassy Lake Enid. The highlight so far has been this seven-year-old by the fire telling me about the movie he's making. In it, a time-traveling dog goes to the past to witness the invention of bones. This outburst of imagination terrifies and shames me, though I know the movie will not be made. When I first moved down here, they told me these pretty sunsets were from the pollution coming off the Gulf of Mexico. I don't know. The water is now purple and orange. There's a small tree frog on my shirt and I'm thinking, boy, I'm really in it. I am nature-casual. I don't love the police, but open spaces like this, where the imagination gets so pregnant, make me uneasy. Grace walked to the bathroom building and, for real, I thought I might not ever see her again. Of course, I'm thinking about murderers. But also, this poor kid who thinks he has a shot in Hollywood. With that script? There is some chatter about whether black panthers live in North Mississippi. They do not. But Grace saw one, lazily crossing Highway 32 in broad daylight coming home from the lake. Is Grace crazy? I think not. We drove separately because a person with the problems I have usually leaves early.

The Three Types of Despair

I've been reading my son's diary for some time. It has been mainly plotless but punctuated by occasional moments of insight. And it's nice when he says something nice about me. Or his mother, of course. The question of his privacy hasn't been brought up. I started keeping a diary too, thinking, if this story helps just one person out there...

Like most, I never asked to be born. But look at me now, a biggish deal in certain small, select portions of this town. Everyone wants to know who my father is, but he did not keep a diary. Or he kept it very well-hidden, because I looked.

I am aware of the exact location of my wife Grace's diary, but its existence frightens me and I do not read it.

There are three types of despair, by the way: being unconscious of having a self, not wanting to be oneself, and feeling that one is not oneself. These are difficult predicaments. These are common anxieties.

On Turning Forty-One

Disaster at the hibachi place. A kid pressed his hands on the grill. The chef cut himself badly. A curtain was on fire. My Grace's drink spilled. The bill included the tip. The saltwater fish tank was dirty. A little girl was crying with gum in her hair. A homeless man asked for leftovers in the lobby. I say this is why I prefer to cook.

Daylight savings hadn't ended and so the sun was still up in the parking lot. What a relief. There was so much left to do and I got a feeling like I used to have in my twenties that goes *let's do this*. It's not necessarily a good feeling, but it's stirring.

A friend once stayed in this motel and saw something darkly out his window he didn't like. A drug deal, a theft, an assault, a murder. He clicked the lock then pushed the dresser in front of the door. The next morning, he moved to a fancier hotel. That friend is not known to be particularly suspicious or paranoid or frightened easily or generally timid or some kind of bumpkin or a prude or a liar. But we're all getting older and more worried.

I say this because tonight there's an art show at that same motel, each room a small gallery. The concept here isn't too complicated. Some of the art has to just lay on the raggedy beds, so you have to crane your neck a bit. They are selling beer and boiled peanuts. They are selling prints. The artists are proud and shy. There's no threats that I can determine.

It's all pleasantly quirky though I don't want a birthday present from here. Last year, I used this day to bemoan what I had not accomplished more than a third of the way through my life, though hopefully not two thirds. This year, the math feels doomed again, no new accomplishments, but my mood has been stabilized.

There have been many breakthroughs. At least, I assume life expectancy is going up, but haven't looked into it rigorously. Once, I was on crutches on my birthday and got a good glimpse at old age. The kindness and the pity—I did give that homeless guy my leftovers. Now the midlife clichés are boringly abundant, the small aches and larger pains. Still, and I hesitate to say *owed*, but I have this feeling, birthday boy, like I'm due for good news.

I did get a present from the art show. A print of our town square destroyed by Martians. I like the concept, the self-sabotage, especially having tried to park there and get to its bars on game day and with all its meaningless undergrads. That's cruel and jealous. In the painting, no one is dying and neither am I.

ACCOUNTING

My father is a retired accountant and during a busy April he witnessed a horror show. At the home of one of his clients who were hoping he might perform some magic and get them a refund, he was greeted by the couple's young son and their new puppy. The son was playing with a toy sword. I'm getting to the part.

Yes, the boy plucked out the dog's eye with the sword by mistake. The eye, still connected, bobbed by the puppy's chin. The puppy *pawed* at it—this is a detail my father always includes when telling the story. The boy began crying and the husband yelled to his wife to please stay in the kitchen. Of course, she didn't, and when she saw the puppy, she threw up.

My father was home early that night, pale as laundry. When he returned weeks later to complete their taxes, he reported that the dog was fine, but lost the eye and depth perception, as well as love for the boy.

I recount this story occasionally, when I think of it, when conversation turns to parents or taxes, but not usually pets. It gets some shocked laughter. If the conversation hasn't moved along, I add that years later, the one-eyed dog was hit by a car and died. I guess it depends on what type of mood I'm in. The moral quickly changes. I guess it says a lot about a person how they choose to interpret this.

We once had a dog that lost her leg to cancer. It wasn't funny. The puppy we have now desperately wants inside the dishwasher or under the grill, an obsession that could kill her if we are not careful. I do wonder if the boy with the sword, probably an adult now, ever tells this story. It would be strange to blame him, but hurting animals is almost worse than hurting people for some people. Maybe his own son begs him for a puppy and he refuses, just leaves it at that.

My father doesn't have many accounting stories as far as I can tell. His other favorite comes from when he was auditing a balking preacher and told him to "render unto Caesar what is Caesar's." That's direct from Jesus, the only time my father has quoted the Bible. It's easy to see his moral code here. Of course, this is the opposite of the other story.

Switching gears, I woke up last night covered in hives, some mystery allergy. I was standing in my underwear in the kitchen while the whole family inspected my riotous skin, pink as laundry. It was embarrassing. I was asked to tell the story of my evening, which I did, emphasizing no exposure to known allergens, no spotting of poisonous insects in the bed. I itched. I had no reason to think my father was lying.

Unabashed

A couple was making love outdoors while a grizzly bear watched—it was a TV show—and I thought, *this reminds me of me*. The romance? The dominance over the natural world? Five minutes before, I had changed a flat tire so fast I impressed myself.

Some believe there are black bears nearby, but I haven't seen one. Come to think of it, I doubt I would be comfortable naked in front of one, and if I were caught, I'd probably snatch my pants before running. Still, the comparison, in abstract, stands. Further still, I don't put myself in bear situations.

I am mainly private, wear socks to bed for emergencies. This accounts somewhat for the lack of followers to my personal faith and for never riding around a room on a chair. I think it's wrong to brag and everything is a brag. It's hard to tell stories.

There is a woman somewhere who thinks my email address is hers. She is looking for a job and I get messages about it all the time. I'm not so cruel as to sabotage her, but I've also stopped politely writing the employers back, explaining the mistake. She could be starving with the lights turned out, but the nature of the problem prevents me from contacting her. I don't get much email otherwise.

Because I'm professional, my email address is simply my name and, somehow, she thinks she's me.

This wedding ring is not private. Tattoos are not private. I walk in contradiction.

Grace said I smell like rubber from the spare tire. I told her she was glue. I have told her only about the fungus under my toenail, but I saw little Chad staring at it on the beach while in flip-flops, which were themselves an embarrassment. It's so ugly. A doctor examined me and suggested a tiny bottle with a tiny brush. Give it six to eight weeks.

I can wait. The thing about privacy is you wait for someone to notice. Maybe intrigue with silence. I hope you're not accused of snobbishness, which is a danger. I have admitted now to my temporary deformity, but that's not the same as displaying it.

When buying a new tire, I observed a dick, a customer, ask the sleepy clerk, "You doing okay, buddy? Out partying too late?" To which my grease-stained hero replied, "I don't party."

As a New Rule, I Don't Miss Things

I remember thinking, *this is the future*, when I saw a whole hotel lobby of people smoking what they then called electronic cigarettes. It was like each had a little flashlight in their mouths, like they were about to do some repair work in a tiny hole. The hotel was old enough not to have rules against this. They were humidifying the place with nicotine and I was jealous. I had just learned, like some ancient cowboy, how to roll my own mess of paper and plant, and here were these...geniuses.

Still, I slept with a woman I probably should not have, but I refused to be embarrassed. I attended a speech by a famous cartoonist. I was just a kid. Another woman who was taller than me flirted the next night, and I thought, *I am legitimately Superman*. I was really happy about this trip.

On the train ride home, I shared the smoking car with five men who had just been released from federal prison. I listened. The sun was coming up on Memphis. None of them insisted on their innocence. It felt romantic.

We all supported each other, regardless of our specific enterprise. That was all years ago.

Today, Grace has arranged to buy a new car. They are going to ship it, though we all know the post office is trash nowadays and you can tell with jokes like these I'm channeling my dad, like getting ready to talk to salesmen.

But there's no haggling and my gags in the live chat are just not landing. We have to accept the car for who it is. I won't smoke in it.

The new car, when it shows up like a bill, will get us to work just fine. But it will be bright blue.

Me, the Kink

Once again with the recurring dream where I am on an airplane that lands on a busy city street and just drives around, wings and all. I have no insight into its meaning, except to say "anxiety," which, in my experience, is the source of all. It's only 4 a.m. and I wish it were 6.

Before bed, the little bats were under the streetlight making big shadows on the macadam. They were feeding, and I was debating melatonin or a request for sex or a slice of that cookies and cream pie. All three could be challenging—best to pick an approach and stick to it—it's getting late.

Unlike most, I enjoy hearing about people's dreams, since it is them at their most powerful. For instance, with me, when I'm half asleep I can see other rooms in the house. This phenomenon is known as remote viewing, something tried by the CIA to see alien bases on the moon.

That's too much, a secret, a kink, a joke to some people. Maybe this is a little more believable:

I've become a morning person, much to the surprise of past roommates, and it's a bit like changing your spots, like becoming type A. It's just a theory of personality and I do like the quiet, just me and my kitchen radio and the fish tank. I feel protective and lucky, watching my sleeping Grace curl her toes sticking out from under the blanket.

I am troubled by the blood on my pillow, the pain in my jaw, the pools of sweat. There's the strange, illegible note I wrote to myself on my nightstand. I am no sleepwalker or epileptic. I am no werewolf. I am not—cinnamon rolls and coffee, that will surprise them. I'll have it all set up for when they wake. We have a flight to catch.

Back Again

I am more afraid of flying than Gabe is, and if I have a vodka soda that might crash my life, so instead I ask him urgent questions about our favorite sports team as the plane rackles and clacks down the runway. I've been told by someone who is not a pilot that there are ninety critical seconds after a plane takes off. Survive that—you're golden—so just count.

My son listens to worse hip-hop than I did at his age, but at least we don't have the generational fight about whether it *is music*. He bobs his head through the cloud ceiling and I lose count after forty-five, thinking of the *three stories* in the last month I've read about passengers trying to *open* the emergency exit *mid-flight*. What a move! When we're at cruising altitude, I let him lift the window shade and he says, "Beautiful," a word only a few thirteen-year-old boys remember.

For his grandparents waiting in the terminal, my son is from a different country and in the future.

Precious time. You are hardcore. It's been fifty years since we went to the moon and once, thirty years ago, I remember seeing an alien at my bedroom window, and saying wait right there. Now, mentally, I know it must have been a trick of the light, maybe some climbing nocturnal critter. But my heart, which can be skeptical and small, has no doubts on this occasion. Like my son, who quotes YouTube that the moon landing was fake, is just trying to get a rise out of his old man.

Asked at a dinner party once to describe the Mothman phenomenon, I said sometimes it is best to think past what you know. And duh, there's grilled pork tenderloin and squash, fried mozzarella with tomato, black rice. There's its red eyes, its symmetrical wings, claws—either believe or don't. Just because they recorded it doesn't make it real seems to be the attitude.

But back to dinner—no, it just got pleasant and uneventful after I shut up, the rain never materialized, the pound cake dusted with sugar was somehow perfect. But google "deep fakes" and tell me that in the future the past won't be made up.

Off that aforementioned plane and back in Old City after fifteen years, somehow it seems safer and more modern, watching the sunlight on the street, awash in free wi-fi. I get historical on my son over water ice. Short Betsy Ross's house is just blocks away, we could barely fit through the door, don't you want to go? It's the Fourth of July in Philadelphia, so I took a photo for some tourists. They called me "buddy" in English. I was happy to do it. Welcome America is really self-care.

Now back home, always *back* somewhere, my coworker is in excruciating pain. Before the trip he was fine, mobile, but now it takes him minutes just to leave the lab. His feet are almost turned backward when he walks. He got old in a week though he couldn't have even graduated yet. We're coworkers but we don't speak—he math, me arts—so what the fuck happened to him? What if he falls? Some comment on his condition seems necessary—his chair has wheels and he's just rolling around!

As you can tell, I'm trending toward more fearful and anxious as *I* get older. The answer is not in the back of the book. Think more: the black widow I found hiding behind the screen door. Still, I'm capable of these ecstatic moments of, like, how far I've come, five hundred and twenty-five miles per hour ground speed. Planes don't crash from turbulence, but lots of people cry during flight.

The Ouija Alone

Rejoice with me, I have beaten psoriasis. There's this trick I have of not watching the news. Most things don't happen, and there's been some debate internally about the order of events. I keep losing things and the obvious answer is that they've been stolen! But the investigation is finished—it is what it is. A black government helicopter is circling, and I'm just reading my big heavy book like that's just a ceiling fan. Our neighbors behind the house, across the gulch, have been growing marijuana. I wonder what for. A family of foxes is our other neighbor. Is there some apophenia going on here? Doot-dee-doo.

What I do is okay, but it's never been prizewinning. I saw my boss jogging and it ruined my whole curbside morning, she further excels. The obvious solution to my mysteries is the Ouija board. I believe deeply in Grace, but she cannot tell the future or reveal what is hidden spiritually. The device is with the baseball bat under the bed.

Today will be better or worse. I can be sensitive and still like football. I can use my turn signal and still be a punk at heart. All this smoke? It's from Grace making simple syrup for the hummingbirds.

What if someone did this to you? Scooped you out of your leaking tank and put you in a cup on the counter? Threw out your old tank but put you in a new one with all the same decorations? This is a little like recovery and exactly like what I did to one of my betta fish. True or not true: there is a world you live in, but have very little awareness of?

This Ouija board is made by Milton Bradley. When Grace plays with me, she pulls on the planchette, and toward "good bye." Gabe pushes on the planchette, and toward spelling "Satan." Use of the board by oneself is not recommended, mainly because of a dearth of energy. We're talking an extra twenty to thirty minutes.

The Witches of Water Valley

They call it Knit Club, I think because of the length of their needles. They convene porch-wise on Tuesday nights, the day of the week most frequently Halloween. Is it true they have a cauldron filled with vodka sodas? Please. Or that in photos their feet don't touch the ground? Hard to say. They aren't that different from you and I. They have tattoos and problems, some even have attorneys (might one of them *be* an attorney?). Their numbers change with the moon. They trade books on romantic poetry and apocalyptic feminism. They paint each other's nails and curse their enemies, which are few. In the winter, they bundle up making it impossible to tell one from the other. In the summer, their gatherings go deep into the hot orange night.

What are these witches of Water Valley up to?

They play no music except when they want their children to dance. The children of Knit Club—feral overachievers lurking in chess clubs and science fairs, on the honor roll and in the principal's office. The women abide male children but prefer the girls, perching camellias in their hair and smearing lightning bugs on their cheeks. Even those without children are good mothers.

All of this is what I can gather from the bushes or out in the driveway. I have not been invited to their dark extracurriculars. Some Tuesdays there must be a banquet; there are dishes left to be done in the morning. Other nights, they feed only on cigarettes and pink wine. Their dogs ignore men, but their cats are many and friendly. And who is their leader, their reverend mother, their queen? All seem capable. That one there once told me, *be gone, dummy, be gone*. That one there actually knits.

Yes, they smoke, can you imagine? In this day and age with their advanced degrees and earning potentials? Their long hair and aforementioned painted nails? Other anachronisms: their steel cups and gypsy kerchiefs and what, from a distance, could only be a leatherbound Julian of Norwich (or is it Anne Frank? Michelle Obama?). They light their cigarettes from an aromatherapy candle, placed at the center of their circle, and ash into the thorny roses that surround the porch. This is not a good place to eavesdrop.

And what would I want to hear? Something flattering, I suppose, some proof that the world revolved around me. I wouldn't be the first skulking man to have this wish. But I can change. I can learn. The porch is their stage in this groundling town. Even the police are scared to pull them over when they leave, even though their blinker is out, their registration expired, their breath rancid with Sémillon.

Still, I've seen these witches on Saturdays, at some child's birthday party. First, they bake, then they sing in their primary-color dresses. When the storm comes and the kids won't get out of the bounce house and the forty-mile-per-hour winds threaten to launch it and the sky is so black it's green, these witches all just close their eyes and the inflatable thing settles to the ground. The rain doesn't start until all the children are back on the porch.

It's worth noting that I live with one of these witches. One Tuesday night, Grace brought a cat home from Knit Club, which was not a black cat, but a brown and white and gray cat. In the mornings, it leaves us dead birds, squirrels, and, once, a rainbow trout. Despite the town's name, there are no cold-water streams here. Only explanation: magic.

Jealousy

I'm hovering around a conversation that's complimenting the size and beauty of this pecan tree when someone else says no, it's an ash. I'm so bored. It's possible I could identify an oak, but couldn't care less. There is, however, this music in my ear, not in my head. I hear it. No one is playing the radio—it's a party.

Generally, other people's kids don't interest me, but sometimes they get involved in interesting things! Take this drunk thirteen-year-old. I don't care how he got that way, but his attempts at deception are entertaining. He exhibits the telltale signs and smells. Now he's hugging the host, his mom's friend. He's slumped on the couch with his mouth open. He's tiptoeing back to the cooler and only I see him. I don't see myself in this little bastard though.

This could take a turn none of us will like, but we're not there yet. I refuse to act because I hate accepting additional responsibilities.

However, I see the kid's point—there's a dullness about these festivities. Maybe it is the heat. What is the occasion?

Finally, here comes Grace, not in a little black dress, but a black dress nonetheless. She's also wearing a baseball cap to change it up. She's—legally—drinking a dragon fruit sangria and grimacing after each sip. Someone at the party is rich or at least fancy and brought it to share. Grace is not the type to pour it out.

"Do you hear that music?" I say. "Are you having fun?"

"I don't, but I am," she says. "Also, did you see that Clyde is hammered?"

That was the kid's name, and now it all made sense. Years before, I had been his youth soccer coach because all the other dads wanted to coach football. Clyde rejected the rule about not using your hands, which made him terrible at the game. Also, after all these years, the thought of what's under her black dress still excites. I'm anxious for that fragile moment when all the guests make a decision and the party is suddenly over. I'm waiting to attempt to unlock Grace's hips.

But young Clyde is a rule breaker, a stance I've lost sympathy for.

Then, the rain starts, and strangely, instead of walking to our cars, we file into the kitchen, doubling down on this party. Be careful—I'm losing interest. Of course, Clyde will be sick, wreak havoc, destroy personal property. But this music. It's like the way a dog must hear with no understanding. I cannot place the tune.

A year later, the same holiday, we are not invited to a party. Maybe there's no party at all. We're watching TV in bed by 8 p.m., and I ask Grace if she remembers the complete chaos caused by Clyde.

"Who?" she says. "I remember Kyle."

I don't love this answer—I remember Kyle too. He had informed the party that he suffered from "climate grief," and touched Grace's hair in a corner of the kitchen. Had his fingers touched her neck as well? I saw what I saw.

What *I* know, what quite possibly I was the first to discover, was that Grace has a spot between her throat and her ear that really sparks her interest. I had chalked their encounter up to clumsy flirting, a small dig at me, the effects of that dragon fruit sangria. I had been dragging young Clyde out of the house into the rain.

As for the music, it persists, louder. It's gotten so loud that I've seen an ear, nose, and throat specialist. He gave me some drops and a cynical outlook.

Deep Play

I just prefer it when Grace is in a good mood, so I'll put my noise-canceling headphones on and tiptoe. A certain fragile stability rides today on whether Gabe makes the basketball team—we're waiting on the list's release. The dogs are not thrilled about the new bedspread. I don't think of myself as a people pleaser. I *have* learned I'm a fan of delivery systems: a gorgeously shaped bottle, a pipe when they come back into style, the Amazon website. I also consider convenience and price.

Kevin thinks he might want to buy our old car, but I tell him about the deadly recall. The red letters I get in the mail say the airbag might explode! I don't want him to try to fix it himself, or doubt our friendship because of lies by omission, but my sense is he gets pleasure from tinkering.

Grace plans on riding in a hot-air balloon later this afternoon down at the ball field. Well, it will not, like, venture forth, just go up and then down. It's for a good cause or something that needs money.

She says, "I know you're too cool for it," but I'll watch.

I have no fond memories of, or sentimental feelings for, the car. It's my fourth or fifth. Once, an eleven-year-old muttered, "Well, this trip just got a lot less cool," when he climbed into the back seat. I didn't even turn the radio on. I let it bother me for about half the drive to see the Avengers when I remembered his own mother didn't love him all that much either.

The hot-air balloon adventure is canceled due to wind. I had secretly decided, yes, I would go up with Grace, but my brave gesture is meaningless now. I swear the next time there is an opportunity to do something with no purpose, I won't rationalize or get embarrassed. Grace says, "It's called 'fun,'" and that's fair.

As I recall, there was a wedding in Georgia, a decade ago, where we danced in an empty ballroom because everyone we knew had left.

Let me think about this further. On our first date, I had to send back a whole plate of food because I was allergic. I could have died, but we laughed and laughed. It's a story we've told Gabe.

He made the team. I'm thankful because he had leveraged his whole personality on being accepted at play. From my perspective, he has decent handles and a good long-range shot. He will not go pro, but that's not the point.

Airbnb (Chattanooga)

This is an easy one. The women were going to run a marathon. No, the women were going to run a tag-team marathon. No, the women were going to run half a marathon. No, no, the women were going to run a 5K. In alphabetical order, they are an activist, an artist, a professor, a real estate developer, and a social worker. I hope I got their titles right. It's for a charity.

I learned the geological term "ridge" from a friend from Knoxville. Tennessee is full of them. Our cabin is at the top of a ridge and so is its driveway, which seems unnecessarily treacherous in the Mazda3. What a view from its edges! Certain death in the Smokies! I mean, there was a lot of hype about this driveway, but of course we made it up and down many times since I'm talking about it five months later.

The night before the race, the cold wind on top of this small mountain was really creating a bad situation. Kevin and I were trying to cook hamburgers, which took about two hours, because, yes, the wind, but also the grill had no lid. While we waited for the meat to at least brown, we talked about what animals we would eat if we got (a) desperate and/or (b) lucky. I kept saying, "They have that at Kroger," which must have been irritating, in retrospect. The kids were in the hot tub with their heads and shoulders freezing, and the women were preparing to go to bed early, folding their running T-shirts, and probably completing the race in their minds.

Twelve of us in the cabin. Can you imagine that? This whole trip was like, *little did we know,* ominous voice. I slept like I always sleep, which is deeply.

The next morning, none of the women won the race, but they said it wasn't important. "It's not a race," they said. Then the kids ran a 2K, mainly uphill. They were pleased with themselves, though none of them won either. The kid who did win was really prepared: expensive shoes, very short shorts, a headband. She looked like a professional having no fun. I didn't like her. Our kids, who I did like, had already moved on, were talking about lunch, while she had her picture taken for some website. Here someone nods and says, kids are resilient.

I taught a class about the end of the world for a few years and the students thought it was funny. They liked it as much as the class I taught about terrorism, the class I taught about the recession, and the class I taught about old books. What am I getting at? I'll take it further: kids like chaos.

On the way out of town, we went to Chattanooga's last real diner. We were its last real customers. On the drive home, they were closing roads left and right behind us. We passed our Kroger and they were locking up, despite a line of customers. Home from Chattanooga, they canceled the basketball game I was watching, and then all sports. The news went dark—not blank, but the opposite of fun.

When Animals Tour the Zoo

I used this time to ask Grace how I could become a better lover. She thought I meant in the bedroom, vixen, but I meant the kitchen. My recipes were stale, my utensils even spotty from the dishwasher. Instead of instructing and inspiring myself, I had been watching a video over and over where a zookeeper introduces an iguana to a seal. The zoo was closed, but I guess the idea was that the animals were bored with no people to watch.

Who could say how Grace might have answered this question, on her terms? Not me of course, that's why I didn't ask. That I fear my wife is self-explanatory. One thing I like about the kitchen is that it is the only place in the house that doesn't have "room" in its title. It could be for anything, not just rigidly bed or bathing, laundry or living.

In these strange times, every recipe seems to require some feckless, troglodytic narrative as preamble. These are about as useful to me as the time spent in the waiting room while my son gets his teeth cleaned. I pace and I scroll.

What this recipe needs is not more storyline though, or nostalgia, or even bacon crumbled on top. In Japan, there is a word for it. Some days, I obviously think if I start the dish early enough in the morning—my lovely Grace strolling by in her pajamas for some OJ!—that deliciousness will arrive. I hate food magazines headlining quick and easy (cheap can go either way). I'm not trying to reinvent the meal. I'm thinking about a decent tomato sauce, a typical chicken noodle soup that cures disease.

I like to see clean plates. I like a full dishwasher.

Grace suggests I come back to bed, the morning light so romantic, the tornado watch still with a few more hours left. She may want to answer my question. She may have questions of her own. And a few more weeks of this and I may be that heartsick reptile not even fathoming the lovely seal behind glass.

Sex Life

Our sex life is often diminished because of our pet dogs. When we were in our twenties, the force of their jealous will was not enough to keep us from each other. But now it's fifty-fifty. There's getting the dogs a chew, and coaxing them into the kennel, the sheet pulled down, etc. By the time we get back to it, we're in our forties.

Other interesting things still happen at night though. Once, while letting the same dogs out late, I saw two coyotes next door play tug-of-war with a housecat. It screamed and screamed and I didn't intervene, didn't say hey, you, lay off. We don't usually have coyotes in town, but I guess here was where the good things were. My own dogs cowered and curious by the door and something ancient must have stirred in them at this sight. But, no, the bottom of the bed and air conditioning and regular pellet meals was still too much. They retreated.

Like the dogs, I have fantasies still, things I won't share with Grace after all these years. I don't know why I keep them to myself. They are not perversions, no big asks. And which isn't to say there's anything wrong with being in our forties, it's just I don't remember our thirties much. But I feel great, up at 6, in bed by 10. It's proper. And there is pleasure, right, in filling the dishwasher, in folding her clean panties and putting them in the drawer. Chill. I've dreamt my love's body was ice cold. I've dreamt I got a really good parking spot at work.

I can be subtle or fresh, but timing is what is really at stake. Best to just wait for what is offered. I once asked a woman if she wanted to screw and she said, "Such language from an English major!" No one gets phone calls anymore, and there's a Catholic side to me too: this psoriasis and bursitis on the same damn elbow.

Grace is at a reptile house, holding snakes. Yes, it's meant to be a metaphor: it's a photo shoot, she's that gorgeous. She asked me to pick up sticks in the yard while she was gone. How's that for something to do? So I'm experiencing a resurgence of lust right there on the front lawn, and still in what I call our foyer. When she calls to say that she's going to be late, I throw out dinner and make a whole new one out of jealousy.

Every ad on television suggests by now I should have problems, but I don't, or don't see that I do. I spent my whole life trying to make it last longer and now there's this. What unfairness. What strife. The dog's bladder must only be this big and the interruptions persist. Most men die with prostate cancer as luggage. I have an energy drink to get the old ticker pumping and turn down the bedsheet.

In my old apartment, we could smoke in the bedroom, which always made me feel like I was in the movies. The heat broke once, just when we needed it. We saw another evolutionary benefit of the act.

Since then, I've seen that housecat alive. What to make of that? The cat escaped? I dreamt the whole thing? Both seem impossible.

That Vasectomy Talk

Grace and I were having that vasectomy talk when one of the dogs walked in, and of course, with him, there had been no conversation. I got the sense that I was supposed to be elegiac. Surgery is dangerous, but I took it as natural that as I get older, I will start to lose abilities, even now, and already. I have already been a father.

I have one memory from the womb: gory, handsome.

I also saw Gabe in his bloody beginnings.

"Nothing will change," Grace said. She was wearing a T-shirt, no bra. I would believe her. Plus, I'm all for change if that's part of the deal. Sometimes, it shocks me that I even still live in this town. I used to like adventure, my history suggests. I've seen both oceans *and* the Gulf.

"It doesn't hurt," Grace said. That sounded nice.

"There will still be pleasure," Grace said, but how could she know, is my body so obvious?

I just searched for "urologists near me" and scheduled a consultation. Probably, I wouldn't have to take my pants off. My Patreon subscribers would love this content. The doctor studied at Penn.

The fireworks were decent at the Watermelon Carnival that night, but there was a heavy police presence. The crowd brought their guns to the seed-spitting contest. We met a stressed-out emotional support dog in the crowd, and we saw friends. My conversation skills were coming back, but I didn't bring it up. Everyone had new jobs to talk about on the patio, and dead loves.

I'd recently been accused of wife-worship. No, I did not say swapping. What would I want with your wife? People are not like—do you remember?—baseball cards. But what Grace says, more than likely, goes.

Still, I couldn't get over the feeling something is in need of puncturing, or of being pinched off, or of closing down.

THE HEART OF A MOCKINGBIRD

I think I'll go for a drive to release myself from the pucker of muck in this archdiocese. No one stuck at home themselves has even looked at my website. The oven, from roasting too hard, is toast. Let us see the turtles with their packed suitcases; the songbirds and cats warring. My phone is too hot to work. Let's roll.

There would be the storefronts closed pre-crisis, trendsetters. There would be the empty new playground, shining up in the rain. That worrisome pack of abandoned fighting dogs.

But my obsessions have returned during this, an ear toward the phone to please god sing. My best friend, 1,200 miles away, has taken to bird-watching, gone silent. We have one, the mockingbird, which will dart from a bush and attack an undergrad if it feels like it. Its speedy heart must just be an on and off switch, what depths could it possibly contain? I don't go for a drive.

Instead, we continue to wait for a part for the oven, ordered direct from Pluto. Grace is handy and I'm perching with this one piece of advice about how to avoid getting electrocuted, bringing sand to the beach.

Last year's garden is waiting for me, but I fear snakes, need gloves. Yes, I've already mowed. I consider strolling the yard like a nineteenth centuryist waiting for a butterfly or brand new type of bossy clover to appear. But, a city kid really, nature has never delighted. I reconsider the car.

There's like this black box I keep pulling ideas out of, each more nervous and mysterious and fanged than the last. In a pile, they form a recent history. See: take a drive, warn wife, garden.

Could there be a little music in the house? Yes, plenty of that. Could dinner be cooked on the grill instead? Yes, that seems doable. Could two friends or family members copy and repost?

NOT HERE BUT NOW

These wrens were building a nest above where our cat sleeps at night. To call someone a birdbrain is a real insult. So, I placed a small mirror in the nest to give them the shock and fear of self-recognition, aka eisoptrophobia.

Some people have ideas about me that are completely wrong. I love that. I don't care that much about money. I like helping people, and I can be good at it. Yes, one of the methods is to present people with a mirror.

Charlotte was always getting stoned and calling her ex, who was me. I'd answer the phone, though I had no interest in a rekindling. Our history together was typical—what began as charming became repugnant. Her affection for me was maniacal. She also stole $3,500 from my personal savings intended for LASIK eye surgery.

Ever since that haunted phase of my marriage where my wife and I swapped stories about past relationships, Grace was obsessed with this missing money. In her mind, we were always about three thousand dollars short of our financial goals.

"You loved her," Grace says. And I say, "If this is love, then that wasn't."

She cried. I cried. We went to *The Graduate* for appetizers and Saint Anthony's Brick Oven for entrees.

The next Wednesday, I was home from work for lunch and I was surprised to find Grace, undressed and in the bed.

"Take me," she said. "I'm a wounded stegosaur and you are the mighty Tyrannosaurus rex."

She never talked like this. I was still wearing my lanyard with my key card, shocked and intrigued.

Charlotte had had a different body type, a different personality, different strengths and weaknesses, different aesthetics, no discernible politics, different turn-ons. For instance, along with the phone calls, she would send pictures. Not selfies, though I think that was the point. Someone else was capturing her at mundane tasks, brushing her teeth, tying a trash bag. Plus, they were not beautiful pictures. I hadn't seen her otherwise in twenty years.

I am not mocking Charlotte. In fact, I'm not mocking anyone.

For the sake of some privacy, which I do deserve, I won't say what Charlotte and I discussed. Grace knows.

And every Wednesday at lunchtime for about six weeks, Grace greeted me in the nude and talking deranged.

"I'm an imprisoned space princess and I crave freedom!" she said. "I'm your high school sweetheart, Rosie Rottencrotch!"

I was enthused, but only neutral on the chitchat.

Of course, when I look in the mirror, it may or may not be true.

The Home, A Desert

By all means find unconditional love if you can, but the dogs can be too much. I have a list of errands to run that are completely invented. I have a place where I smoke that doesn't allow pets. They have their cozy cages. Grace is busy or asleep.

I'll say for now, it's unclear what is terrorizing me. I have spoken to something I shouldn't. The anatomy of some mornings is gross.

We painted two rooms—blue and white, respectively—and the house still smells of turpentine. For a day, we all had headaches and short hallucinations. And now my son, Gabe, enters the picture. We painted his room blue, by request. We strung LED lights on the ceiling, by request. We leave his thirteen-year-old self mostly alone, by request, though the room is lit like some sort of sex den and his grades are falling. It's clear he will be a handsome, probably successful, man once his anger calms down.

We painted the new home office white—Grace taped and I rolled and Grace used a small sponge on the corners. It's fun for only about half the time. The impulse now seems to be to fill the room with plant life, art, and surge protectors. Dalí's *The Temptation of Saint Anthony* features prominently. Have you seen it? A naked Egyptian, armed with a crooked wooden cross, fends off spindly-legged elephants, among other demons. I chose it for its realism.

Cont'd to-do list: reorient. Arm yourself, mentally.

Grace came into the kitchen last night holding a baseball bat, saying, "What's the deal?" The deal is protective, not sporting. The deal here is we agreed, no guns—Gabe sleepwalks. The deal is the painted house should be kept safe and knees could buckle and jaws could even become unhinged. I could swing it.

I reminded her of the deal and she kissed me. It was not a come-hither kiss. She said, "I thought I heard something under the bed and there was this."

The baseball bat is from when Gabe played little league, a weapon for a five-year-old. The gun I want is the Mark XIX Desert Eagle, I think, used by the Israeli military and popularized by many rappers. I have no idea what makes it a good gun. But, mocked as I was, I did not spend this morning pricing DEs ($1,800). I put snickerdoodles in the oven for the dogs. I wipe my hands on my jeans and think about buying an apron.

Athanasius wrote about Saint Antony and so did Flaubert. Breughel and Bosch also painted him. He is most famous for his fight with demons, but he did other good works.

The Politics of Water Valley

Having come back from a specific brink, conversation was difficult. They were talking about the art gallery and I asked, "Well, how much does something like that cost?" Victory, I was ingratiated, though not in the market. It's station-keeping, I thought, sometimes you just need the right username and password.

Then our state senator walked by with the town's largest watermelon on her back. She had won an auction at the fair and was looking for a knife. Our simpering president, I used to be able to speak about him, but this is much better. Her plan was to divide it up, like reverse votes. Here was porch-worthy discussion, right: the best way to slice a melon. Now find a way in.

The psychiatrist, no, her nurse, said I'd been taking a juvenile dose. Let's up it. That way things will seem more lighter. More filled with light, my head a balloon full of good speech. Can I afford not to? I'd become so blank in company, a coat rack in summer, an airy aquarium. The trick with the pill was to take it and never stop taking it or else things will get mega-real, i.e., bad. I just want to be chatty.

So. So many things to see at the fair. Vomiting children, homemade pickles and whole fried onions, hermit crabs with Confederate-flag-painted shells. There's a tower to fail to climb and the actual antique car that triggered climate change. Why be so negative and elliptical? Exorcize your first amendment.

The state senator found her knife and began slicing on the hood of the car. My pocketknife had a small melon baller but she refused it. She did thank me for my vote. Our conversation ended when the line started to form: free watermelon!

As night fell on the fair, the creepers and dark preachers from the county arrived. They rarely provoked city limits, but they wanted their measles-positive kids to see the street dance, and they wanted to compare their homemade tattoos with ink needled in a shop. They said nothing, just rolled up their sleeves. They had heard rumors of the free watermelon but grew their own anyway. Battling prayer groups formed and mainly they fought among themselves.

All this seen and intuited from the porch. I brought up the art gallery again but there was less enthusiasm now and the crowd had been drinking. Conversation was random. One participant was crying without consolation. This was not, like, the Art of the Deal. Sometimes it feels like a long time ago that I was a good person, that credit maxed. And not having friends is lonely, yes, but also embarrassing.

Aural, Gestural, Spatial

Rejoice with me, I have beaten mania. There's this trick I have of lowering the bar. My student athlete, Wes, is sulking because I won't tell him the answers to this quiz question: "The conductor of an orchestra primarily uses this mode of communication: (a) aural (b) gestural (c) spatial." There's a number of problems here, not the least of which is that I don't know the answer. Also, Wes has never been to the orchestra, nor does he have any great sense of what a conductor *does*. Of course, these are some of the things I like about Wes.

The weather is homely. The weather is lonesome in winter here. No songbirds or thunder. The window above my computer is just a gray sheet. We left our holiday lights up, and because they are up, we leave them on.

Quiz failed, Wes leaves sore with no inclination to google "orchestra" or wonder for even a second longer what the word "aural" might mean. I am filled with joy. I'm waving my hands in space and, like, whooping. My job is sometimes just cosigning what people have no interest in. It's okay, Wesley.

I do hope one day Wes goes to the orchestra and feels the power of the baton on his own terms. Regardless, on the last day of the semester, it will be summer, and we'll mock the professor together.

When I find Grace in the hallways of the house, she is calling out her phone's name. She has her hands cupped around her mouth like she is deep in some wooded valley. If there are degrees of being lost, the phone is only slightly—she just had it! As a professor herself, she knows everything else about the world, except the location of her phone.

I call her to help and it rings somewhere.

My Wife's Phone

Got laid. By Grace, so there's no shock or scandal. But not before I helped her find her phone. She swore she had it when she left Colleen's, but now here she is crying in the carport, phoneless.

I imagine when Grace dies—I've seen this in movies—I'll hug all her clothes in the closet, smelling the perfume I gave her. That's how attracted to her I am.

This is not to say Grace is sick or involved in danger.

Sex is not a thank-you card in this house. The phone was, almost inexplicably, on the bed.

Infamous

My friend rear-ended a horse-drawn carriage, and that ruined everything for him for a bit. There's a lesson here. The animal was not hurt, but a crowd formed and really *lambasted* this friend of mine. The horse, of course, was in the wrong—the driver of the horse. My friend has guilt, but no crime.

Kicking through leaves in the kitchen this morning, I thought I should get my friend a present after I pour some coffee. To cheer him up. Many years ago, there had been sexual tension between us, but it cleared up, that fog burned off. Someone should sweep this kitchen too.

But what does one get for a person who is bedridden with embarrassment? My friend believes all of Water Valley is still talking about his accident. He believes he is the opposite, negative version of famous, for which there is no word. Neither could I think of the appropriate gift.

A different man once said to me at a barbeque, "I love this weather. Girls in summer dresses," and it felt like someone was looking through my medicine cabinet.

I said, "You fool, that's my wife. She goes to sleep to the sound of dogs growling. She also already hates you."

"That's fine," he said. "Did you hear about the asshole who crashed into a horse-drawn carriage?"

"No," I told him. "No, no, no."

Some days—it's so sad—all my wife has for me is directives, but I defend her honor. Just like I do for my son who rides the bench—he's just a sophomore! He has to pay his dues, I've heard. Just like I do for my friend who rear-ended a horse-drawn carriage. His vision at night is not great, and his astigmatism distorts the lights into halos!

Full disclosure: I know the horse as well. One afternoon, it appeared in my rearview mirror, and as I slowed down, it galloped past my car on Highway 7. I was doing the speed limit—the horse had escaped.

Kind, Heated House

This cat has shown up at the house, very vocal, very bossy. It's as if the spirit of someone my family has wronged inhabits it. People don't believe it gets cold in Mississippi, but winter is gray and rainy and damp. So we feed the cat. It has a big head, so a big brain, so maybe it's pretty smart, which I respect. I've never really seen a cat I'd consider to be pretty.

This is off to a strange start, a sort of dead end. The cat bit is about kindness, but I'm not always this way. I don't, like, enjoy sitting on a bench in the cold listening to an elder talk out their wisdom. I get more from music with no beats and no words. I don't always read the entirety of your emails. There were a few videotapes I didn't rewind. The ice maker makes little frozen bullets, which could be a metaphor if I felt like talking about how I used to drink too much and was unkind.

But Xmas is coming and I've got a little money in my pocket. A first. It's really Grace who is the gift giver: she has the depth of imagination and is good at the internet. I tend to give people what I want them to like. Unfair. Once, when Gabe was little, we made him watch a video where Santa said he could have done better this year. We had chosen the wrong script, but Gabe still remembers the fear. He's standing in the kitchen now, tall as me, still not having a laugh about it.

It's well-known that the day's first cigarette is a good one, and some mornings I just don't feel like feeding that cat. It costs very little, but it does cost. What had the cat done to get itself into this predicament? Where is my upside? Grace, of course Grace, has ordered a heated box for it to sleep in. She sees the whole transaction differently.

But, oh my god, I am not having a moral crisis here. The cat—black and gray, bigheaded, like I said—will move on. It is well-fed. Cats, I've discovered—and this can't be true but I heard it from an expert—don't talk to each other, but have learned, through kindness, to speak to people.

O Names in the Grass

It's my birthday again and I'm putting gas in the car when a specter from grade school looms, Brian McSorley, though I've changed his name for reasons you'll soon see. He greets me, tells me he's a cop now, and that if he were in uniform he'd kick my ass, freak. I'm forty-three years old today. I am not transported to memories of being bullied because we had been friends, and in general, I was well-liked. I share a version of this rationale, and he evaporates or walks back to his car.

The weird thing is, I don't even live in the city I grew up in, and Brian didn't seem the type to ever get out of the neighborhood, and I'm still pumping gas, and is it even my birthday? I'm neither free from trauma nor bothered by my history with this dude. What's with the ghoul?

It *is* my birthday. When I get home there are presents and vanilla ice cream cake, which is just fine.

Gabe announces that he and his friends broke into the field house at the ball field and found a bunch of spray paint. Grace and I don't support this. He says they just painted their names in the grass, which will soon grow and be cut, no big deal.

We rarely discipline Gabe, more like philosophize at him. We tell him, you better hope that grass grows, and was he dumb enough to sign his full name? This is about as close to nature as he gets. Grace lays out the standard claim that our town is policed, though at work I preach to my students the concept of self-policing as a habit of the professional and mature.

The town is small enough that the man I've identified as Brian McSorley will probably make another appearance, but not in what I want to accomplish here. I'm the tiniest bit famous here for not fitting in. I know a few lawyers if my ass ever does get kicked.

Speaking of, the puppy is making his move to become the alpha in the house, assuming it's still fashionable to think dogs organize themselves in this way. He's pissing everyone off. My alpha trick? Walking calmly through the grocery store with Gabe among all the panicked, lost dads because we know these aisles by heart.

PLEASE NOBODY

Even medical tests bring some joy. There are many types of sadness, not the least of which is the type that brings pleasure, you sad sacks. Look here. The cat is healing. After just one dose of this white, antibiotic powder, the wound is closing like a mouth.

I was thinking negatively about fireworks again, about how they are the normalization of war, about how we were all watching *the drone* film the fireworks instead of, like, being *in the moment.*

Can you believe someone who thinks so negatively can have a happy brother? I can. I worked on it.

"Have you noticed I've been less critical about things in general?" I asked Grace, who was shuffling her gender-neutral tarot cards. I was happy to just listen.

"You have been cooking more mediocre meals," she said. "More grilled chicken."

And there you have it: you can practice being less of something.

But what was in the cards for me?

An ex-lover called to say they had their wisdom teeth out, could I provide succor? Hell no, but I went and watched a movie there until the pain drugs put them to sleep. I snuck out with the cat staring at me. I was nice, but not too much.

A friend once prepared a fake valentine for me because I was bemoaning. Again, exactly what was necessary. No one was in love with me that way.

But once, the fire alarm went off in a hotel in Memphis, and Grace and I were on the street in our pajamas when another man suggested Grace go back to his room instead. She slapped him, while I was asking the desk clerk about my computer.

Everything is going perfect in my life right now. Please nobody move a muscle.

Airbnb (Mobile)

There's a haunted parking lot where people go to end their lives, and I've been to that Walmart. I make a joke to Grace and don't even get a chuckle. There's something on the bottom of my foot that will need to be looked at, after I ignore it for a few weeks. Looked at by a doctor. No one has flirted with me in years, probably because of conditions like this, I'm always limping. But not complaining—it's fruitless and a bummer for everyone. I bought the wrong crypto with no research but I'm going to ride it out. Today's guest speaker says, "They may not like me, but they don't respect me either." Yesterday's guest speaker said, "At sixty, I can run faster and do more push-ups than anyone in this room." I've seen the speech for tomorrow and he'll say, "I pity medical doctors because they spent twelve years not making any money." But keep your secrets, Mobile, I thought you'd be prettier. We advanced on you, open-minded, but definitely three out of ten. No one really cares, but I swear I'm doing excellent work. For example, my reply to the sunset over the bay: that's crazy.

Learn for Her

Let me think about this. If Grace hates Valentine's Day does that mean I should ignore it or make it extra special? Bear in mind, she's not the type of woman you can just give *Hamilton* tickets to. I had a mint for lunch and am not thinking straight, but I'm holding onto the air in my mouth for a kiss. This is no exception. I drive to the Dollar General, then turn around and go back to work. Not the Family Dollar—the other one. The algorithm is recommending I listen to an album of the noise icebergs make. It is not, like, *surprisingly musical.* O Grace! My love for you has turned glacial, formerly more like lava. The clerk had been taking away the boxes of chocolate already and exchanging them for shamrocks. I was too late. How about I learn for her, learn to iron? How about I file our taxes? My students think they are clever because they believe the holiday to be a gimmick to sell cards. Some are virgins—it comes full circle. A day to celebrate Grace and love? I can click on a gift, for sure, and be sensitive to her habits.

Justice

When we were introduced, I said, "That's funny. I sat next to you last weekend at Snackbar."

But he said, "I haven't been to Snackbar in years."

He was a very specific type of goof. And I do have the ability to recognize people.

"You wore a green turtleneck and brown sport coat," I said.

In fact, last Saturday, he had been sitting with a much younger woman, I want to say a graduate student. The awkwardness between them was not sexual attraction. I had been eavesdropping because I had ordered poorly, and was bored by my plate.

He shook his head and looked at his wife. "Nope."

His wife was interested. "When *were* you at Snackbar?"

It seemed I had reintroduced a bone of contention between them, so the couple drifted toward the opposite corner to argue. I was not a part of any evildoing. And, remember, telling the truth about bad behavior doesn't make it good.

We were all at this poetry reading—the poet was from out of town and competing for a job. Every other person in the room knew the hiring would be internal, and he had no shot. This insight seemed to dawn on the man during his third poem, which was an extended metaphor about the dangers of microplastics. He suddenly looked embarrassed and terrified. It was heartbreaking, but, yes, kind of poetic.

For myself, I find it difficult to worry about microplastics. Given my medical history, something else will surely take me out first.

As for what I overheard the weekend before, the man had been giving a dull, cultural history of our small town in which he played some minor role or witness. The young woman entertained his lesson, nothing overly excited.

I had ordered red drum in a state of panic when the waiter arrived, the menu was that uninspired. Nutritionally, it wasn't a terrible choice, being low in saturated fats and calories and a good source of calcium, protein, selenium, and niacin. But the dish wasn't more than the sum of its parts, and the butternut squash purée presented as baby food.

At the cocktail hour, the poet returned again and again to the bar. I was checking on him from across the reception. He looked dazed and a little drunk. Just a reminder here that this was technically still part of his job interview.

I had wanted responsibility, but I didn't know it would come with all these responsibilities. For instance, I'm the poet's ride to the airport.

I lost sight of the first couple. I may have ruined their marriage.

People these days don't have the common courtesy of disappearing from your life. You can always be found out.

Fervent Waiting

No more with the game plan where I badmouth everything I do, think, and feel. For instance, I sexted Grace and she wrote back, *lmao maybe later in the week*. Okay, see, a line has two sides, and time, it's been proven by scientists, seems to move faster as you age. This was not a no. Later in the week? That will be here soon, and also gives me time to prepare (flowers?).

Still, I'm showy-mad and so withhold a compliment I've been working on for a bit about a small part of her body I find perfect.

Meanwhile, Gabe is still sleepwalking. Once he walked past me in the kitchen and peed into the heating vent. He peed in the fish tank, which had high difficulty. He peed in his closet, in our closet, in the closet in the guest room. The irony here is that he is too shy while awake to make this happen at rest stops, at friends' houses, in hotel rooms. I tell him to picture an enormous glass of water pouring into another. I tell him to think of the sound summer rain makes. I quote insight from my radio-youth: free your mind and the rest will follow. But he continues, crossed-legged, red-faced. My heart breaks for him.

As he gets older, the list of things I cannot do for Gabe will get longer and longer. This is not a unique parental realization though.

A week passes. I make chana masala, which had medium difficulty. I don't go to Sonic for an ice cream cone every night because I recognize my tendency to obsess. I buy Grace some succulents.

My student athlete, Wes, calls me wanting to brainstorm paper topics. Due tomorrow, morning.

"Sharks," he says.

"Too junior high."

"Gatorade," he says.

"Too commercial."

"Legalized weed," he says.

"Already happened, pretty much."

"I'll call you back," he says.

"I believe in you," I say.

Wes just needs a C. He's cool with a C, and we'll get it. This weekend at the game, he'll stay on the sidelines, but remain looking ardent.

Wood Street Idyll

Shots fired on Wood Street and a scared-looking kid ran across our front lawn. Grace says she's calling the cops about the gun, but not on the kid because she doesn't want him killed by police. We think we live in a nice neighborhood, but what does that mean? That our neighbors have a collection of wind socks and chimes on their front porch?

If I were a different storyteller I might have met the kid later in another context, befriended him and gained his trust, found out what was going on with that gun. Gave counsel. I gave my own son an early birthday gift instead.

Chain-smoking now on a nature walk around the back yard, looking for rare wildflowers and trying to uncomplicate these feelings. I have three rules, none of which apply here. We have a door that could be easily kicked in. I am craving sunlight and craven.

To say I've been hassled by the police is a stretch. Once, I was called "Tupac" by an officer at a roadblock because of my tattoos, but usually they just let me go with my fucked-up registration.

I'm reading a book about how the stegosaurus managed to have so much sex. The point is all those spikes on their backs and tails, but you can find their bones everywhere. I'm also reading a book about the deep future, the coming wars over the Arctic and the best windswept plains. But I don't feel doomed like I used to.

I once watched this NASCAR driver crash and flip and in the interview afterward he said, "Winning is one thing, but when will this all end." I feel his sentiment.

I'm still in the back yard, looking at the house. I believe, for no reason, that the kid and the gun will not reappear in my life—every hour it seems more like a dream. I sweareth, here among these bright red wasps, violence cannot be an answer.

The Cannibals of Water Valley

Coming out of the gallery, I was thinking I want to hear the sky. Was I so moved aesthetically? It's a dumb thought, right? The art was good, but I was mainly impressed by the artist's financial decisions—no loans. Our neighbors, the graduate students, also cannibals, packed up all their stuff and moved overnight. They always looked intellectually famished. Sadly, they have a little girl, and I bet, as man-eaters, there wasn't a single painting hanging on the wall in that house. There *was* a preacher who would sermonize from outside their front gate on Sundays. Regardless, it's all falling into place. With the cannibals gone, it's just us and the artists on this street, and I'm cooking chickpea stew beneath a print we bought, and the sky is mainly quiet. We do eat meat, but not tonight.

After dinner, I think I might bring up the idea with Grace of committing a crime together. It would be our powerful secret like when she was first pregnant with Gabe. It would be fraud, not obvious violence. I believe in this idea. I'll say, "Do you think we need more money?"

Jeweler's Row

Rejoice with me, I have beaten depression. There's this trick I have of remembering that my mother used to carry gems in her pocket as a teenager. No thieves suspected! This is more biography. She and her friend were making deliveries on Jeweler's Row!

Despite her early training, my mother did not become a gemologist, instead a lab tech and occasional phlebotomist. Some of her friends call her Blondie.

Grace prefers emeralds. Once in Charleston, we picked out a ring for her birthday, and if I follow the memory, we walked a long pier and looked at Fort Sumter, a Yankee and a Rebel in love.

Someone I know stole this jewel detail about my mother when I held it out to be admired. She lied and applied it to her own life, which really would have been impossible by then, the city had gotten so dangerous.

When I got my ears pierced at twenty, the girl at Claire's was impressed I didn't flinch. The holes are still there if I ever get rich. See below.

There's a dog missing in town and the reward is $5,000. Her name is Ruby, which is not a lie meant to enhance the overall theme, but rather, reflects the breed of the dog, a redtick hound. I don't know where the dog is, but it occurs to me that searching for the dog might be a lucrative hustle. If I were to go looking, I'd put some treats in my pocket and check the dumpster at Sonic. Eventually, I'd check the highway's berm, which doomfully attracts dogs like a magnet.

Of course, Ruby has been stolen. Her picture on the posters shows a beautiful and desirable animal, no doubt, capable of love one could not put a price on.

Clean, Slice, Inflate

There are some questions, like, who is this Colleen person? Are you in love with her? What's the backstory here? I've gotten into it before, but it's enough now to say she holds a place in my life. In an emergency, I guess I could call her.

Of course, I'm not in love with her. That would be Grace. I mean, she brought peaches to the house that were clearly nectarines. Loveable. Her shoulder is frozen above her head, but she's doing her exercises. She cannot send me the email I really want though. Nobody probably can.

But Colleen needs to borrow our wet vac—I don't remember buying it. She wants to borrow our mandolin—it terrifies me. Also, our air pump. Her plan is to achieve things this weekend. Grace and I say sure, sure, we weren't planning on slicing our fingers open this Saturday.

The house is emptier.

Sometimes I worry Grace cares more for Colleen than for me. For instance, she won't let me borrow her toothbrush. But it's the kind of petty worry that serves no purpose, is without ground, confuses. To make up for it, I overcompensate, and write down for Colleen all our passwords, and throw in a novel too.

I go back and forth.

With all that stuff gone from the house, Grace and I have room to spread out. The kitchen is now wide as a dance floor.

When Colleen returns what she borrowed, there's a bandage on her finger, of course. Could she please borrow a summer dress, a strong flashlight, and two tablespoons of coriander? We have these things too! We are pretty helpful. We're not even annoyed.

Disagree and Commit

Connor, who doesn't really interest me, made a discovery. His wife, Colleen, left a dirty note from her lover in her jeans pocket. Oh boy. She knows Connor does the laundry.

Where do I come in? Nowhere, really. I am not the lover! Grace is on Colleen's side. They are friends and Grace believes that people—women especially—are entitled to happiness and adventure. Connor is so good at laundry that he flips everyone's socks and checks everyone's pockets.

Colleen, busted, insisted for a moment that she had written the poem as an act of self-love. Connor is not a forensic detective, but that's clearly not Colleen's handwriting. Grace has read the poem and said it wasn't very pleasing aesthetically, but, hello, was it raunchy (plus, rhymed).

When I say Connor doesn't interest me, I mean that in the nicest way possible. We say hello about 75% of the time in the grocery store, but now I know all the things he's not doing to Colleen.

And who is the lover? This—poet? Colleen won't tell, so he, or she, has become all of us.

Meanwhile, I'm working very hard to make this one restaurant *our spot*, for Grace and me. I bought cologne that purports black vanilla. I secretly borrowed a book of Henry Wadsworth Longfellow poems from the library. Report: he's not filthy at all.

At our restaurant, Grace asks what I think of this whole Connor and Colleen difficulty. I want to say I am cheered that people write love poems anymore—suicides are up. But what comes out is that it's a real creep who writes poems to another man's wife.

I had also ordered too much food and worried about the bill.

Grace believes that marital status does not change one's ability to inspire a poem, and she told me.

I'm thinking about, not to mention, its pornographic nature.

"Not to mention," Grace says, "the identity of the poet remains unknown."

For Grace After 9 p.m.

I feel like a princess in a story waiting for Grace to come to bed. And when she does, it's as exciting as seeing myself on TV. No one else knows this thrill, which is thrilling. This is not really about sex. Tonight, as usual, I say, "I feel like I need a weapon to protect this," and she says, "It's still early, but I'm so tired." Then she is snoring, which is a good sign. Some nights she has to turn the TV on and wrestle with something. I get up and check the front door, which is already locked.

I had thought there weren't really enough hours in the day to cheat, but then I witnessed what's going on with Colleen and Connor. They were raising their voices like it was time to leave. He was quoting a poem he wasn't meant to have read in mixed company. She was basking in its words guiltily. This is all happening at a PTO meeting. They each had two margaritas, so, four total, and the tequila was making them aggressive and sarcastic even though they ate dinner together. Connor said, "'Your legs are honeyed pathways to bliss,'" and Colleen said, "Don't stop, coward." I mean, it was a total mess.

That Connor had memorized the poem from his wife's lover. That Colleen was newly turned on. That the vice principal kept talking about the raffle. When this is all over, the couple will be divided up among friends, each calculating who has the most power and who deserves the most empathy. A butchery.

After the PTO meeting, I baked forty-eight cookies. I had volunteered among the tumult. I took out the trash. I snooped in Gabe's room for drugs. I made a big deal out of all of it, kept clearing my throat, so Grace would notice. Don't leave me. And if you do leave me, don't cheat. And if you do cheat, leave no documentation. This is dedicated to everyone who has ever driven in front of me, seeing in their rearview, the speaker at his most vulnerable.

We Don't Encourage Stopping By

When Gabe wouldn't talk as a baby, oh man, did we have excuses. Same as now. Colleen wants to know where we've been, have we sided with Connor? She's at the door in denim. Our house was built in the fifties by a man's man but we have a woman contractor now, which we like on principle only. It's a pain point for us, all those voicemails. But Colleen has dipped into the pills she takes before flying, and she's like slurring her growls. Grace and I stay quiet, let her talk and question—accuse—she's been through it. Though, of course, she started it. Poor Connor, who reminds me explicitly of an elephant, stripped of its tusks, deciding to trample a rickety, abandoned village. This is exactly his reaction metaphorically out in the world. I'm not going to say he's hiding around the corner in the kitchen. He's not. We are trying not to get involved! Instead, Grace and I have inserted a new move into our lovemaking—we just made it up. You have to keep it fresh and awkward or else you end up like Colleen and Connor. Other than this moment, no one ever comes to our door. We don't encourage stopping by to borrow some sugar. The dogs hate it. I hate it. Grace takes a step out into the carport, thankfully. Some might think I am obligated by gender to take Connor's side in this mess, but I haven't since 2018. A person with pink hair was flirting with Grace at the movies and I didn't even get mad or punch them, though

Gabe wanted me to. With Grace and Colleen in the carport, I go back to the kitchen, where Connor is in fact hiding. "She has denigrated my manhood," he says. "It's tattered." He has the look of a dog that's been mounted. "People should lose their jobs for doing what she did." I pour him a soda water, and then Gabe walks in the kitchen, already talking about basketball. I don't want my son to see this. "Do you have a girlfriend, little man?" Connor says. "Watch your fucking back." I'm training Gabe to look for love and beauty in the world and this ain't it.

Swamp Fox

What she did was so trashy and criminal I can't even talk about it. I feel like a dog watching an airplane. It's come up a number of times. There was also betrayal. The whole town is going to have to figure this out, if it comes to it. It's also none of my business. We're just sitting around talking shit.

Further, the local kids are lighting bottle rockets from between their teeth, but Gabe is with his grandparents, and I think, even if this goes the way I fear, it's not entirely my problem. It's a holiday. Grace is splitting a magnum of champagne, and we learned that the neighbor's dog we thought was shot was just hit by a car. There's the sense in this country, or at least in this back yard, that things are improving.

We just got back from vacation in Charleston, and we told stories about it. The octopus carpaccio, the steel Atlantic Ocean, that good 5G. Fort Sumter like a garbage barge on the horizon. We had to leave town early to avoid the parade.

On the drive home, fireworks still going, Grace is talking about the Swamp Fox, a South Carolina hero. I'm emphasizing here that she is buzzed and happy and thinking about revolutionary history. In my own northern education, I learned nothing of this man, can't contribute. He was a guerilla, but our guerilla apparently. On a fountain in Francis Marion Square, it read—and I took note: Is it the truth? Will it build goodwill and better friendships? Is it fair to all concerned? Will it be beneficial to all concerned? Presumably, the Swamp Fox speaks from the grave!

But, no, this is the Rotary Club motto, the builders of the monument. It's a fine conversation starter, and one that should have been taken to heart by the woman who disgraced this town. Marion remains silent in the muck, cheating at war.

At home, the dog that hates fireworks has destroyed the brown couch, her confusion and anxiety is that prevalent. There's no point, they say, to punishing a dog. God bless them, they seem incapable of regret, or are, at least, reluctant to acknowledge it.

What I preferred about Charleston to our little town was that no one seemed to be from there.

A Feature or a Bug?

Grace directs me at dawn to get donuts, and it's like *everyone* got laid last night, saying, "Good morning," and walking their dogs. Ah, to be loved, to be learned, to be lurking about. The donuts are so unnecessary—I feel rich buying a dozen—but it's a good start to a bad day, since Colleen and Connor will be visiting. These friends had been flirting with divorce, but then they were in a car accident and a pedestrian was killed. Now they are trying again to make their marriage work—it was not their fault.

"We aren't murderers," Colleen says as they cross the threshold. They aren't elegant company—Connor especially with his webbed toes and sandals. "No charges were pressed, remember," he says. The jaywalker was to blame, but this is an unsettling greeting. Grace had said just that morning that she felt, not like a host, but rather, a crash test dummy.

Colleen and Connor had been going to couple's therapy and used these sorts of visits to try out their new perspectives and techniques. Connor, for instance, had jealous rage. Colleen too had the rage, but of a different sort. They now tell the story that the accident that killed that young man really brought them back together, assuaged their rage, and provided insight into the nature of love. Grace and I were suspicious. The jaywalker's teeth had been knocked out of his mouth.

I didn't cook, or even slice anything, for our guests. Grace won't sit. The history of our friendship with these people was getting foggier and foggier. After sneaking away into the kitchen, I say to Grace, "Remind me how we know them."

"There was a time," Grace says, "when we enjoyed having drinks with Colleen and Connor. Before they were married, they were fun and also pleasant. We often played trivia at the bar, and even went on a beach trip with them once. Connor is a good dancer, and Colleen is a dermatologist. Then you quit drinking and were in the hospital, and they got married and resentful with each other. Connor found a love letter from another man, and Colleen didn't do much to calm him down about it. They were in a terrible car accident and someone lost their life. Now, here they are."

Is it a feature or a bug of adult friendships, their presence? This isn't the first time they've used our living room as a sort of stage. They did have the effect of making Grace and me feel perfect.

"You know, Connor is building a tiny boat inside of a wine bottle," Colleen says. "Very meticulous work."

"It's a *ship*," Connor says. "But, yes, it takes great care. Did you know Colleen is writing poetry now?"

"That's efficient," Grace says. A car's tires screeched farther down the street and the couple flinched.

"What do you like about Grace?" Colleen asks. No doubt this was therapy-speak, and I feel, for their own rehabilitation, I should try to play along.

"Grace once threw a meatloaf off the back deck into the yard. Her parents were over for dinner and they claimed it was too salty. We had to order pizza."

Larry Young is the name of the deceased pedestrian. He had not been drunk—just careless trying to cross the street between two cars. Colleen and Connor now have the nerve to believe he sacrificed himself for the health of their marriage, and it made me uncomfortable. If Grace is right about our previous friendship with these people, I just could not recall it.

"Another thing I like about Grace," I say, "is that she always texts me when she's getting a pedicure. Like, she's at her most comfortable and still thinks of me. I also like the way she smells in the morning."

Colleen and Connor stop playing along. They get up from the couch.

"He," Grace says, "always writes in blue ink? Isn't that cute? And he never exercises or complains about not exercising. And he wonders if every rock he finds is a meteorite."

They were creeping closer to the door, gathering their things, their new car throbbing in the driveway. I still had a kind of amnesia. Even their names are escaping me.

Airbnb (Birmingham)

Okay, the joke is all the drivers do is turn left, but tell that to Gabe, who wants me to explain downforce, which, I think, is what keeps the cars from lifting off when driving at 200 mph. We're going to Talladega! This is a gift for all I've put my son through.

The night before the race, it's prom in Alabama and all the seniors are at PF Chang's. We are at PF Chang's, waiting amidst the disappointing and precoital cologne for a table. Grace orders a martini from the bar with a chunk of ginger in it. She doesn't like it, ignores it, but I think, *give me a shot*. Two years before, I would have paid it very strict attention.

Arriving at the rented apartment, I had expected the host to welcome us, give us a tour, check us out. Instead, the key is not so cleverly hidden in the mailbox. Inside looks like the night before a sophomore might move in, everything futon. I keep waiting for the owner to show, gloat, check IDs, though Grace assures me that it's not how this works. The trust here is incredible.

In the morning, Grace drops us off at the track, and will meet friends for a day in the city. She has never in her life expressed hatred for NASCAR, though many have, and she'd have the right to from back in the bedroom with the engines growling on the TV. My own feelings are ambiguous, channeled direct through Gabe's body into mine. Grace waves goodbye.

The atmosphere pre-race is like some Deep South Constantinople bazaar. They are selling car tires and jewelry, tattoos and turkey legs. There is Joey Logano's crew chief giving a talk about viscosity on a stage. There is Austin Dillon signing ball caps. Logano is filthy rich and half my age and appears regularly on Disney+. Dillon is more likely to wreck than win, according to my son.

I'm anxious, so we find our seats. We are fans number 53 and 54 at a speedway that holds 110,000. The track is so big we can't see the other side of it. It has its own hotter weather.

When the cars start, it's like someone has turned on a garbage disposal in my chest. All the men and boys take off their shirts and take out their vapes. The woman behind us, unbidden, starts applying sunblock to my son's neck. This is it!

We take a bathroom break at lap 100. This goof in the concourse wants to know if there's any beer in my backpack. I tell him, apropos of very little, "I'm here with my son," and he says he won't start any shit since I'm with my family. There is no beer in my backpack. Even when I was drinking, there was no beer in my backpack.

Eighty-eight laps later, Kurt Busch is the winner. His brother Kyle is universally hated but this we are okay with. We begin the half-hour walk to the highway where we will be picked up. The trash is in piles and airborne. The fans are sweaty and sloppy like the track has blown its nose. My son retells the story of the race and makes it seem more exciting.

Meanwhile, Grace is circling on Highway 78 until they reopen the exit. It's getting dark and the fluorescents are going out and the cops are leaving and my phone is dying. Out of the dark appears the ghost of Richard Petty, who is not dead, but needs a ride. We point in the other direction. Gabe is scared. I think how beautiful to get back to that shitty apartment and have three cold club sodas.

There's like this irony to being a liberal at a NASCAR race which is only minimally interesting and I'm trying to resist. There's slightly more drama if I say, bear in mind, I used to drink too much.

I'm Up! I'm Up!

This was real life and she was actually showing a group of teenage boys how to blow a bubble. I also happen to know that her JavaScript is excellent. I do have some gum, but this is no place for me. The youth is shocking, and this wasp has been in my car for days, by which I mean I'm in a bad mood. The yoga did nothing. The teeth whitening, nothing. That trip to Yazoo City, boy, did we go. I have a picture in my camera roll of their witch's grave. Maybe I blame that. I'm in the Yazoo City of the soul, hack hack! I've always imagined the soul as a pair of glowing lungs. That's too much. I'm in the Birmingham mall of the soul, spending green money on Gabe. It's actually quite mild—in this mutant food court, we are smiling and superior. Grace asked where I would go if I had five days to myself, and the right answer was nowhere without you, but I said New York to work and Tokyo to eat. I've never been in a hotel alone. I'm so bad at reading her mind.

Bored, There Was a Rainbow

The power had been literally out for two hours and I hated playing cards. In the dark, that thing where I cleared my throat a hundred times got really annoying and I was not having a moment of communing with my pioneer ancestors. I was reading *The Changing Light at Sandover & Zombies* with a flashlight in my mouth. It's not that scary. But with storms like these, people lose their minds/trees, the roots end up pointing up. The psychological effects, for me, are mild—this house has brick integrity and our magnolia trees could be taken down a few notches. There was no appliance buzz, and it's like I'm hearing our home for the first time. The panting of the dogs mainly, their scratching. This natural ambiance inspired me to be romantic.

"Come kiss me under the rainbow," I said to Grace. "There's a rainbow and just a drizzle."

"Not now," she said, "I'm engrossed in this word puzzle."

It was at this point in the dark Gabe chose to realize something.

"I was an accident, wasn't I?" He was learning Calculus and Sex Ed and combining that education, and for that, our pride continued.

So I said, "Like a rainbow is an accident," which was not the right thing to say to a teenager or really accurate.

"Happy accident!" Grace yelled from the bedroom and Gabe laughed as if we had just unlocked his freedom to do whatever.

I kept trying to work the rainbow into conversation. This showed I could be socially awkward when I wanted. "I'm going to take a picture of this rainbow if anyone wants to see."

No one did, so I didn't.

The birds came back. There were trees we wanted and trees we didn't want, but none were damaged. There's a young oak I wouldn't mind dragging to the curb. The magnolias, it's illegal to cut them down. I remember Mrs. King frowned when I just pruned one. I'm allowed!

Then, Gabe asked, "Also, am I circumcised?"

But, what luck, the power came back, cramming the rooms. I nodded. It, all of it, was a *non-issue* now. This was just a little afternoon. We'd lose these soon—Gabe had been packing his bags one item at a time for years. Grace might invest more ruthlessly in her puzzles. It will become hard to distinguish which memories have value. They'll continue adding ghouls to books. I am not that old.

I Had a Chauvinistic Thought

I had a chauvinistic thought while mowing the grass, but decided to keep it to myself. Working 7 to 4 can do this to people. Cut, the yard somehow looks worse, but I'll call it a "lawn." There's also the sensation on *the lawn* of walking on trapdoors, thanks to the moles or mole. I flipped the mower too, very dangerous. I'm supposed to feel some American-type ownership here, some pride. Where is my lemonade, Grace?

Yesterday, long story, I was reading from the town's Book of Wills, printed 1913 AD. Very eye-opening. The wives dole out the family jewelry, and the husbands describe their tombstones. This is not research for my own will, which doesn't exist, I will live forever. It was a request. I was told once I have a sexy voice, though I can't remember by whom or why. Still, it helps me speak.

The problem with the grass is ticks, and the problem with ticks, of course, is horrifying disease. They line up where my underwear starts. They think they own the place, but really, they are parasites. The moles don't really bother me, the little gravediggers, the little graveshifters, the little mortality-reminders.

I met two women who said they had never seen lightning bugs until they came here. It must have been hard to believe, since most insects annoy. But I hate when they get in the bedroom at night. Do they think their glow is sexy?

In my fantasy, Grace is watching me out of the kitchen window, my biceps flexing to push the mower up the hill. The sweat looks good on me, the droplets. That we can conceive and luxuriate in these types of thoughts is a miracle. I am much sadder out there to look at.

I think it's wrong to call things Sisyphean—that guy really went through it—but, yes, the grass, technically, is already healing, growing back. It's Monday.

I'll Say This Then I'll Shut Up

It is true that there are too many guitars in this world, all the strumming and plucking. Grace puts on Lee Montgomery or Bob blabbermouth Dylan and it's like she's trying to hurt my feelings. "This is American music," she says. We're sort of enjoying each other's company in the carport. A stray cat we feed is obviously sick and so there's this moral dilemma. Not every animal in this family gets an automatic, expensive trip to the vet. He may just have to tough it out—there are limits to our compassion. The cat is just licking its food. Grace says, "Fine, you pick a song," and this never happens. I look at my library for five minutes, trying to make my case, and choose something made by a musical algorithm. It has no heart or social critique, but plenty of if/then programming. These days I'm after a sound I've never heard before. The sick cat's name is Valentine, and he doesn't know we talk about him quite a bit. He *is* worrying us. Coincidentally, I bought a new shovel. Grace doesn't like my music now, though I courted her with songs years ago. My father once dealt with the strays tearing up my mom's garden with bowls of antifreeze. They cannot resist it, though, of course, it's poison. He's more of a dog person. When I bought the shovel, I was thinking about removing the holly bushes in front of the house. I was thinking about restarting my own garden. I was thinking every house needs a quality shovel. Valentine, who used to be bossy, is in decline. We don't know his history, medical or otherwise. He's on the hood of my car, very likely suffering. Grace puts on a song from our youth, a compromise in our argument. It is "Holidae In," a song so fun and stupid, and about as deep as a dinner plate. The lyrics come flooding back to us. These days, we do enjoy getting a hotel room, two towns over. It's like a fake vacation. We order fresh baked cookies after ten o'clock and the delivery person sneaks down the hotel hallway and knocks quietly on our door. It feels luxurious. Grace might even take a bubble bath and drink La Marca. In the mornings, we spend $40 on donuts. What the guitar says to me is *I've run out of ideas*. What Valentine says to me is *Help*. What Grace says to me is *Babe?*

HER HEALTH WAS GENERALLY FINE

But Grace called saying she thought, maybe, quite possibly, though doubtful, she was having a heart attack. I was about to leave work when she said, no, wait a minute, that's it, it's over, I'm fine. I didn't feel great about the last fifteen seconds, but I wasn't a doctor. I said call me back. There was a small part of me wishing for an emergency, I admit it. I wanted Grace safe, but a surprise day off, the adventure and company of a waiting room, interactions with health professionals: this all sounded A-okay for Tuesday. Does no one else feel this way, with this terroristic imagination? The glee about the busted water main, etc.? Now you want to know what I do for a living, and do I have insurance. Reunited at dinner, Grace says she believes the pain and discomfort came from an air bubble in her chest, though there is no such thing as this diagnosis. I don't care. She likes this little story, and it's better than dying young or being scared of being startled. The consensus remains that she'll outlive me, thank god.

Grace's Melancholy

I remember when Grace picked out this new floor for the kitchen and her dad said to me, "You're not going to like it." I thought it was so-so. When they pulled up the old floor, there were dinosaur bones and mice. The coincidence that there was a ceratosaurus skull, complete with nose horn—my childhood favorite—made me think this was an intervention. But we took some pictures with it, then sold it to the Water Valley museum for green money. The mice don't bother me and remind me of college. Who goes there?—my former roommates! Shout out to Olney, Glenside, Fox Chase, Jenkintown. These are all places in Pennsylvania, where I was schooled, where the only bones we found were of the boring, frond-eating hadrosaur, and those of my friends. But ceratosaurus was a hunter, fast as my Mazda. And if you want to see it, just go to the Water Valley Natural History Museum where it's shined up like a shark's tooth on a necklace you'd get at the beach.

But Grace is sad. The dinosaur money is spent and the new floor doesn't look as good to her as it did in the catalog. She won't step foot in the kitchen during the afternoon when the light from the sun is just sprawled out. She thinks I spend too much time at the museum on weekends, as if I were a painter. Work got busier for both of us. The only time we're together is when we pass each other on the internet.

The first thing I say every morning is "Stop"—speaking to the dogs—but it's the mice that are eating the dog treats. Feeling lonesome, I've accused Grace of posing around the house with no follow up. "Stop," I say, "or go." The natural history between Grace and I is long and romantic, but last night she said in her sleep, "I'll never get to be anything again." It broke my heart, though I don't really know what she was talking about. She can be whatever she wants! Again and again!

It's hard to be entertained. I am not always entertained. I spent $300 once to be bored. Now something has slipped out of place for Grace. She's trapping the mice in no-kill plastic boxes. She's thinking about Weight Watchers. She got depressed reading an article about tree equity. When we found the dinosaur skull, I thought we were making, like, *beautiful music.*

Woe Is Grace

It's blue outside because of the snow, and this storm is a hyperobject, which I've learned means it is too large for the human mind to comprehend. Grace's depression is a hyperobject too, though Gabe and I have produced a small circus with the dogs for her enjoyment. It's 2 p.m. and she won't budge from the bed. The dogs love the snow. Even Gabe, a gnarly teenager, is enthused. But when I tell Grace about this miracle in Mississippi, she just mumbles, "K." If you know anything about depression, she has the type where nothing is really wrong, or can't be solved with a little effort or help, or can't be ignored with a little distraction. But that's the problem. The bedroom window looks out onto the back yard and the dogs are frolicking and Gabe is throwing them the ball, and the snow, and Grace won't even peek. Our marriage could sustain this, but would prefer not to. I took her to dinner and she ordered the dumbest, whitest fish, though they had garlic snails and sea urchin and gizzards or livers. She drank two Svedka martinis and furrowed. Then, she would not button her coat on the walk to the car though it was freezing. Oh Grace! I'm trying not to be inconvenienced by all this—it's not about me. Though, I am now sadder too by proxy. I'm shoveling at night. If I thought her love for me was truly in jeopardy, I would encourage something to be prescribed. I have my own, and the pills are little hyperobjects. There's a hawk in town—we should all stop what we are doing. Like a real hawk, a bird. The snow has melted, so if I could just get Grace to look up. The little dogs, other people's dogs, are freaking out. It was on our roof then took off! But it's not far. Everything is a hyperobject once you learn the definition.

GRACE COMES OUT OF IT

Things should happen faster. I feel like a puppy following the sunshine on the carpet. Then, Grace is up at 6:30 a.m., wanting breakfast. I get potatoes, jalapeños, onions, tomatoes, and sliced cheese. I grind and brew coffee and set the cream and sugar on the counter in bowls. I mean, I'm the one who's supposed to be depressed. It's about as erotic as breastfeeding, depending on your opinion. She eats the whole meal, says she's feeling frisky, then flashes me. Will I have to think of her in a new way? Will she see colors differently, more vibrant, more colorful? And will I remain enthralling?

Vouchsafe

This dog was abused, I think, and that gave it a shitty personality. That's the correct cause and effect, right? Otherwise, the story of the dog is much sadder and I'm just trying to cheer up Grace. Her long sadness had broken, and she appeared, bath-bomb-radiant and pink, excited to attend a movie? I cannot stress the deep dejection she had previously felt—don't say wet blanket—and moods are a type of muscle, stronger with use. I'm not an expert! But I told Gabe to go pick some flowers while Grace and I talked about the type of story we'd like to see told. Because we had never planted any flowers, Gabe came back with some handsome weeds, and no one fussed about the difference if there was one. It was a new day, but fragile!

There are, of course, multiple frameworks available to choose from. I am not sitting. I'm trying to pet the dog even though he doesn't like it. I feel that if I can just keep the dog from barking, the situation will resolve. Otherwise, all is lost and we're back to the beginning, the bottom.

"This one sounds fun," Grace says, and I go with it.

"Grace!" I say.

"What?" she says.

I was so happy I felt like buying presents, but then again that thought occurred to me that I am the cause of all of Grace's misery. I'm becoming more nonprofit. Last night was not my best meal. What movie?

Gabe interceded. "Pizza," he says.

We came home from the movies and the dog is still growling. It's a hustle keeping Grace—up. Which is to say, keeping up with Grace. It's the movies where she regained pleasure, and so we've seen everything we can in English. Even so, there is that horror that it might return, that darker Grace, and contagious. We have this pass that lets us walk right in and the carpet is, of course, red. They know our order. I've read the disease is lifelong and I still plan to find out, though these tiptoes on the sticky floor, my own swirling anxieties and obsessions and occasional tics. And poor Gabe watching the whole time, seemingly happy if fed, growing like a weed. He approaches the window of onset. We must be invited into his room.

To think, Grace recently championed the installation of a "Slow Children At Play" sign on our street when just last year she used that funny word about herself, lugubrious. Worse than that. I have been imagining the family breaking up like a band, sadly working on our solo projects because of creative differences. Now, she's thinking civically because the cars were coming by so fast. She's even thinking romantically: a matching bra and panty set. She still removes my hand, but the progress is undeniable. As for my own mental health, I'm cruising.

Grace Is Foxy

I wonder if there aren't two stories here.

One is probably getting the sense that my wife, Grace, has no problems of her own and is the sole voice of reason in the house, but that's not necessarily true. For one, she is up for tenure. She's also struggling to read without glasses, grinds her teeth while sleeping, and has a fairly persistent and unaccounted for spasm in her pinky. I mention that she is *not* in a wheelchair because she has recurring dreams that she is. Her tooth enamel is famously failing.

I find her holistically foxy. It can be hard to compliment someone without objectifying them or criticizing others—everyone wants in on everything. I'll say, she would be on that game show if only our internet connection was faster, and she'd win. I'll take Grace in a bathrobe. I'll take Grace in the passing lane. I'll take her pedagogy and her good and bad tattoos.

This is a character sketch to keep in mind when I describe what I'm going to do next.

Foxy, But Wrong

I have some evidence that I'm sensitive: I can feel an email coming five seconds before it dings into my inbox, and a whole graveyard once told me to "Move along." As such, I have not undertaken lightly the decision to allow my son, Gabe, to use the Ouija board with me.

Can't follow Grace's judgment here—and Gabe begs and begs. My only concern is this: I read a warning that said please don't use the board if you are sick or debilitated, and of course Gabe's spleen was bruised in the car accident. At Christmas, I find it difficult not to get Gabe everything he asks for. In fact, most days.

I feel googled. Grace knows my intentions but can't police every minute. She has just forgiven me for the last time I betrayed her better judgment. She hates the music I listen to, thinks I use too much salt. But I dress in the clothes she bought me.

The purported danger of using the Ouija board while "debilitated" is demonic possession. But Gabe is thirteen and curious about his future. He's old enough to keep his soul safe and his mouth shut.

WOMEN LESSONS

I am married to a woman who once came home from work and fixed a Diet Coke and champagne. No announcement or explanation—I watched her crack open the can, pop the cork, and pour.

"Twenty years together," I said, "and I never really knew you."

"You're so traditional," she said. "And, in that sense, neophobic."

That hurt.

*

I once worked with a woman who claimed to be the heiress of the Dr Pepper fortune. Some ancestor of hers had invented the recipe and sold it to the great Coca-Cola Company. She told me this while folding T-shirts, which is also what I was doing.

"Peach," she said. "That's the secret."

She was probably twenty-five at the time, a retail dinosaur to my mind. Her name escapes me, as does her face, and the name of the store where we worked, and the reason she eventually got into a fistfight with another employee and lost her job.

*

I once drank with a woman named Taffy in the Hard Rock Hotel and Casino in Las Vegas, Nevada.

Eventually, she said, "Do you want to go up to my room?"

"No," I said. "I'm with my friends."

Ricky had discovered that if you sat at a poker slot machine, the waitress would bring you gin and tonics. By then, my full psychology and physiology was dedicated to bourbon, but free is free. Taffy left. I started talking to this grizzly bear in a V-neck sweater instead, but he didn't want to be new friends, he wanted to sell me drugs. I still entertain the idea that Taffy was actually a murderess. I still entertain the idea that luck and intuition are fundamental forces.

*

I once blacked out holding hands with a woman in the hospital. If you've ever had surgery, you've met her too. We had a very intense relationship that lasted ten minutes. She saw me half naked, then sensed that I was nervous. She put something yellow in the IV, which was really great. I felt emotional. I was in love.

She didn't tell me her name. She covered my mouth and flipped me over.

*

Every day, I speak with a young woman at school who is unmotivatable. Privilege is not her issue. Lack of god-given talent or skill or time is not her issue. Cruel, vertiginous migraines might be her issue. She is not in love with money. She is not even in love with life.

She arrives late and leaves early.

*

Every year, I eat brunch with two young women, my nieces. Sriracha honey fried chicken and waffles with pepper jelly. Heirloom grits with goat cheese, chorizo with scrambled eggs, fruit cups with mango, dragon fruit, and melon. Iced-down orange juice with a pull-top. Mugs of black Kona coffee, and there's my wife splashing Diet Coke into her Prosecco.

It's always so cold, even though it is Spring Break. We take in the art in the hotel lobby and ride the glass elevator. We cross the bridge by the waterfall. It's possible that this will be the extent of our relationship going forward—there is no blood between us. But still, I have an unexaggerated sense that should they need me, for whatever, I would try to provide.

This Is What We Trained for, People

Is this all because I was caught masturbating as a kid? I think not—I refuse the trauma. The world's best restaurant is closing and I've never even been there or heard of it. I'm learning the personalities of the Board members and they have their own problems. There's a point I'm trying to make, but I'm on vacation.

Zoning out at the Hornets game and Carolina doesn't love its team. I'm here for slam dunks, but the DJ won't quit and I can't hear the players' sneakers squeaking. He's playing "It's Raining Men," my mother's favorite song. He's playing the "1812 Overture." He's playing every song called "Money," and there's a lot.

There is a man—though one is tempted to say "child"—absolutely losing it over a fried chicken sandwich in the concourse. He did not get his way, or his way did not come fast enough. The world, we learned, revolved around him. How surprising! Here, we thought it spun about us. I have this look I can give that means something like drop dead, and I do give it to him. It's two days after Christmas and you can tell that some of the people in this stadium just learned that Santa Claus isn't real.

On the train ride home though, everyone is comparing designer shoes. The passengers are looking good and experiencing fidelity. This is, to some degree, what it's all about. Be honest: do you watch the game or the scoreboard?

Wes's Betrayal

Wes has cheated! He plagiarized. He bought a paper online about, of all the banal things, the dangers of playing violent video games, and I'm so depressed. I am confused. I am heartbroken. I am also a suspect in the academic integrity investigation. He will fail the course. He may be kicked off the team. He may have to leave school altogether.

We've been told not to speak until the investigation is over. I am professionally lonesome. I had given Wes the best of me, and it was not enough!

When he calls me late at night from a number I don't recognize, all I can say is, "Why?"

"I was running out of time," he says.

I knew this about him, that he struggled with time management, but I didn't think it was this bad.

When the investigators come for me, they have one question: have I ever indicated to Wes that it would not be possible for him to complete this assignment ethically?

I told them, "That would be counter to the positive reinforcement that I'm famous for."

I'm back with my other fourteen students now, Ashley, Desean, TJ, etc. My heart is not in it. I let them choose their boring topics about the benefits of recycling, or their polarizing arguments about abortion. I adjust their commas and format their Works Cited pages. I try not to bring the mood of my work home with me.

Timorous

There's an intersection by my house where I know one day I'll have an accident. You don't have to see the future—it's only a two-way stop. My prescience fails when it comes to just how injured I will be. Will the car be ruined? Will I have said a proper goodbye to my family? Can I afford this? It's possible that every day I drive through the space where I will be killed. Thinking like this is somewhat exciting, adding an extra complication to my days, which are otherwise pretty straightforward.

For instance, there's this technical part of my job where I look for a specific cord for half an hour. The building is filled with cords, so many cords, but the right one? Close at hand? The one that fits? No, never. The point is the effort—I'm modeling behavior. Then we're all searching for the cord together, splitting the rooms and closets among us, hunter-gathering. What we find, of course, is an adapter.

Is it cowardly that I slow down at that intersection? Adjust my behavior even though I have the right-of-way? I'm just in a Mazda, waving my hands, when truck after truck blows the stop sign.

He helps make them, so Kevin is describing what allows a bullet to fire. There's this tiny indentation, a tiny amount of very dangerous powder. Sometimes, at his work, the dust builds up and—pop!—dozens of bullets are fired with no gun. Mainly, it strikes me that he'd make a good teacher.

We're in his garage because there's the type of rain that makes driving nearly impossible. The temperature is dropping fast. Fall is coming, like, tonight.

That Aspect of Happiness

Tornado watch, and there was no violence at the robotics competition, no flame-throwing, no gears clattering and rolling off into the warehouse. Friendly nerds, in the sense that they like to build things rather than buy things already built. They comfort me. It was seventy-five in February, but wouldn't be for long, arches of clouds were surrounding the valley. Fooled, the mosquitoes and crickets woke up and were at the windows. This is nature writing in the transcendental sense, my out-of-body experience during the semifinals, the theme: people versus creation, oftentimes the bitter cold, but today the storm. Everyone should have a good twister story— the weather is so nervous before it really picks up. Hours before, they asked me to give a speech during opening ceremonies, which I nailed with no prep. Then things went wacko. See here, there was a playing of the National Anthem before the machines revved up and maneuvered, while a ninth grader admitted her love for someone in eighth. There was no line yet at the concessions stand. I felt—some bliss. I couldn't feel myself in my Nikes. The display of imagination and fine-tuning was remarkable in these young people, and it truly knocked me out of my life.

It wore off. Even the tornado watch expired with no drama or even rain. A team I had no fealty to won the championship, and I had that post-epiphany headache. That aspect of happiness that is bored crept in. They were rolling the credits at the robotics competition and I still had to lock up. I said my congratulations and the winning driver said, "Never forget who you are."

That's fair. I used to, I suppose. Now I try to remember, though I had just seen the future.

In the speech I gave, I said it was so wonderful to see young people reject virtual violence and embrace teamwork. I said in the coming days we'll need ... I've forgotten. As I said, this was all top of the head. This is me, signing off, after an experience of the uncanny.

Yolobusha County Idyll

It's that time of year where I cut myself with the knives I got for Christmas. By accident. As gifts. It's early baseball season. I heard high-pitched thunder, which is an absurd description, but accurate. The whole atmosphere reminded me of the time I caught my dad laughing in bed. I could be lonely.

I was not alone. In fact, I was speaking. I was making an elaborate suggestion to a high school class about their futures. I had a crystal ball as a prop. I was clutching my business cards. Their teacher called for a round of applause and I didn't get one.

Then, of course, I was stuck in their mud in south Yalobusha County between Grenada and Coffeeville when I encountered an angel in a motorized wheelchair. Every life decision the two of us had made led us inexorably, messily, to this exact conversation.

He said, "I need a new hip."

I said, "No. I'm stuck."

It's at about this point in the story that most people expect the man to drag my car out using only the small engine on his chair, but sorry. In fact, the most interesting part has already happened. The rest just took a long time.

As I suggested in a roundabout way above: it is just now spring. The drive home on the spare is straight and smooth.

The prediction of rain has been delayed. The tire pressure light on as it should be.

But look at these cuts on my hands! Did you know I was so tough? That one there is all black!

That man in the motorized wheelchair is talking about me—this is not an idea of reference. My nose is actually itching. Maybe, it is some of the high school students, considering my advice. Regardless, I'm thrilled. Why should I not get the attention I deserve?

The Future Is Not Urgent

When asked, she said she wanted to be a surgeon, but then admitted thinking about all the stuff inside of people made her feel weird. This was, of course, at the County College and Career Fair. I said, "But what about software development?" and she flitted away. I've been nothing but kind to you. I'm two months off Lexapro and I want my erections back. The future is important, but not urgent.

At home, there is a note taped to our door, addressed to "Neighbors." It's from our new neighbors. We haven't met them yet, and already, they are bossing us around. Can the tree trimming truck park in our driveway? Can our dogs stay in the house when they are having romantic dinners on their patio? Can we live *better* since we're so close to them now?

Had my first genuinely psychic experience the other day, and I'm proud of that, always learning. Also, I saw a fox cross our street at night, but surely, it meant nothing. When I locked the facility at 4:30 on Friday, I said to my colleagues, "This is peak weekend, the whole thing is in front of us." My narc had had nothing for me that day. He walks so slowly to make the day go by faster.

That night at the homecoming game, there's even a cheer for when our team takes a time out. It goes, "Talk it over, Big Blue, talk it over!" My son gets #69 face painted on his cheek, and I wonder, what does the future hold for you? We lose the game, and this is not what I had in mind.

Monday at the City College and Career Fair, and where are the culinary schools, the poetry schools, the schools of thought? There are tables for the community college, the Army, the Navy, the Marines, and the Air Force. Also, the tire wholesaler who does $1.5 billion in business right here in our past-obsessed state, and you want to design video games?

And so nauseous from withdrawal. I'm sitting here with my little bowl of pretzels. I'm drinking an Ensure and smoking a cigarette. I called out of work and realized the house is blessed with so much good morning light.

Prostrate

In the dream, she fell from a ladder a few stories, a tall ladder. I did not see the impact and assumed someone would call 911. Not me—I got the heck out of there. I was guilty of something, or at least feeling guilty.

The next night, returning to the same dream, she is bruised, in a cast, limping, scabbed, but too dazed from the fall to realize that I abandoned her. We are back in good standings, even kissing. There is nothing to forgive.

Awake, and for the past few weeks, I have forgotten to be handsome, but it's not like my wife has a device to see what I'm dreaming. It's not like I can control these things, the brain chemistry. I've been losing weight to the metaphorical cancer in me. I have figurative diabetes, literal bad breath. I have been unkind, so I'm baking her favorite. I'm dropping off the recycling at the substation. I'm studying her wish list. I was, what? A jerk. A whole bouquet of orchids won't save me.

Does she dream violence for me? Or even crueler apathy? She is a black box, even after all these years. I touch her broad back at night. I whisper a joke she's liked before.

Closing the Board

I won't bore you with the details of our Ouija session. The spinning chair, the apparent date of my death, the terrible screeching from Gabe. Gabe is fine. He's laughing now.

Grace is at Colleen's, drinking wine and complaining about work at their private picnic table. When she texts me, I'll go pick her up.

All is quiet now.

The light in the bathroom dims halfway through my adventures in there, but the bulb is old. The scuttling on the ceiling must be mice.

I do not, on the small scale, come from a history of violence. I don't pick fights, right?

Gabe is back in his room. Like others have said, I'd give my life to spare his. But he's getting older now and can heft some of the family burden too. Back when he was born, I held him, then mixed a drink.

I have forgotten to close the Ouija board. I'll do that now.

Seven Years

Grace is watching the show about that bad addict and they're screaming and it brings up bad memories somewhat. After all those years, I don't fantasize about bourbon, but I do dream sometimes about being institutionalized. In it, there's a painful helmet I'm required to wear to fix my brain. Life is good now, easier. It's unclear if Grace sees me in this TV show, but that's her own private, mental life. There is a reptilian part of *my* brain that lights up still when she pours another glass of wine. I guess this anatomy would have to be removed with a laser for it to stop.

All of this to say, there's a lot of yelling on TV these days. I've stopped watching the news and most other things and this decision is contributing to my new happiness. Am I hiding? Ignorant now? Better than well-informed and fucked-up and sick. There is one show I like about a fish out of water. There's another show I like about when a stranger comes to town. Grace also likes the one about going on a trip.

Listen, my coworker often says. Listen, before she starts to talk officially.

COMMISERATION

That we are in decline, if not bottomed out, seems obvious in the macro. But I, here, have been renewed, rising with some speed, happy. I cannot make sense of it. Even Gabe, in his miniature weight room, is literally getting larger, taking up more positive space. Am I supposed to be gloomy? I even stopped for a turtle in the road and moved her safely on her way out of harm. What happens next will be up to the she-turtle, but I can't help but think I've done my part. I was given a raise also.

Fast forward, and Gabe and I are watching the Indianapolis 500 like experts, like engineers. He has picked the winner with thirty laps to go, and he will be correct. Grace says, erotically, "I'm going shopping for a bathing suit," and out she goes. I hope she gets an expensive one.

This country is again in mourning, and also the whole planet, and there was even a bad house fire down the street from my work. That enormous flag at the community college is at half-mast, almost dragging in the parking lot. My own situation is not in tune. *We've* rediscovered the pleasure of mixing iced tea with lemonade, cinnamon with milk. The days are longer, and the music I listen to is getting calmer and calmer.

Would it be more appropriate to be sad? I'd have much more to say—I've been struck dumb with felicity. Yes, don't get it twisted: I have come close to being tragic, but this, right now, is a small-g golden age. I know the world will infringe, take something from us, spit, maybe soon.

For instance, I just saw a picture of myself with gray hair. The doctor said use this medicine for the rest of your life. I abuse my heart.

Grace returns from shopping, pleased. Just so you know, she is covered in flower tattoos and sunburn, but did not get a bathing suit. I'm grilling a farm-raised rabbit and spring asparagus. I'm smoking my favorite type of cigarette, which is getting harder and harder to find. I'm making plans for as far ahead as next weekend.

Gnashing

Grace, let me know when you're ready to talk. I went to a poetry reading about crystal meth and depression last night while you were at Colleen's, and the only thing I could relate to was that it was in English. I am clean. I am happy. It's almost April and it's like soldiers are marching home.

You're teaching a friend to be more academic now, on your own time, which is nerdy as hell. Gabe has brought his grades up—all As and Bs. Wes—my protégé, my lieutenant—has apologized using his non-university email account.

I wanted to tell you that Gabe walked in on us last night when we were getting down to our business. Your back was to him and your eyes were closed, but I looked him right in the face. I wanted to tease him about it this morning but got suddenly terrified he might say something hurtful and off-color.

The birds are tweeting this morning, what-the-fuck-was-that, about the storm last night.

You suggested I try this cream below my eyes, not because of the gray bags there, but rather, to experience its cold activation effect. I'm on to this, but will consider it. Truthful, delicate suggestions are one of the advantages of marriage. I've applied it now.

Minimal damage to Gabe, I'm sure. But it was the first night in a while I had trouble sleeping.

Someone was tweeting about what makes for a good poem, so I suppose they knew something. I disagreed in private, remembering the best that have been told often cut off three quarters of the way through with no satisfactory ending. The conversation turns left and happily.

There are also the violent epics, which we still talk about or at least allude to.

Be a dear and finish up with your work. I also want to tell you about the two young men who keep walking past the house, obviously casing it, obviously goofs, obviously trouble of some kind. These days, my love for you is so open and convenient, I could split their heads if they stepped foot on the driveway. These men in shorts in winter in our front yard: try me.

But no, no. My mind is clear waters. I might at least gnash, but this duo are just lost kids, looking for love, jealous not of my TV, which is huge, but of the capital-K Kingdom.

Dear Aggrieved Friends

Over the past two days, three of my seven betta fish have died. I've sent them to the sewers. Last year, I had a dream where a betta fish told me what to do with my life. Awake, I couldn't remember the answer, but began collecting these fish around the house in one-gallon bowls. The advantage of this particular type of fish is the myth that for some reason they don't like the things other fish do, like clean, fresh water, a full belly, or much room to swim. You've seen them for sale in pet stores trapped in clear Dixie cups. The females are drab, but the males have long, colorful fins. If two males see each other, they fight until one or both of them dies, so they need separate tanks. Probably somewhere, cowardly gamblers bet on this small bit of violence.

The average lifespan of a betta fish is three to five years, which isn't very precise, and it's hard to say how long they were on the shelf at PetSmart before I brought them home. When they are dying, the color drains from their fins and they tilt at the bottom of the tank. It's very sad. A healthy betta male spends most of his time thriving at the top, building an optimistic bubble nest, even though he has never seen a potential mate in his entire life. Hope springs, etc.

My son's betta, Your Worst Nightmare (ironic that he named him this since I did not tell him about my dream), was among the casualties. He was bright orange and rescued from the dismal pet section in Walmart. My son didn't grieve. We also have three dogs, now a cat, and a Venus flytrap, and so the death of this fish registered about the same disappointment as noticing that his shoe was untied. They say kids can be cruel. But after my son started sixth grade this year, he pulled out crates of his old toys. The screens are powered off, and he is down on the carpet arranging dinosaurs in battle. He is positioning cars for a great race. Surely, he is mourning something, if not the fish. He has that capacity.

Our most extensive sex talk occurred at the Sonic drive-thru. Gabe already had a clumsy understanding of the mechanics of the default act, recess chatter. It was mainly the accompanying slang he was confused about, and for the most part I could help with that. Also, the why of it all baffled him, as if he now, at eleven, held the instructions to a machine whose use was mysterious. Like, why would two people do these things to each other. He's just in the sort of intro swamp of puberty, not yet in over his head. Like, it's probably time for me to buy him deodorant.

I'm old enough now to know people who are divorced. They sometimes say such terrible things about their exes, anger being a symptom of grief. But most are better off without. Two of these divorcés are at my house right now, sheltering from Hurricane Michael on the Gulf. They were supposed to get married to each other this weekend on the beach, but the storm is not romantic. They are not taking this mess as a bad omen though—their wedding was going to be small, cheap, since both had done it before. I wasn't even invited, but now here they are in my living room. They'll just do it another weekend. Mainly, they are worried about their new house and all their stuff, which is, of course, a totally legitimate concern. Their marriage though—that'll be A-okay.

For about ten years, I've been working on a poem that goes like this: "I hate the fucking / beach." I've found nothing to add, though I've thought about that line break and am still not completely sold on it. We went to the beach just the other week, and I thought the trip might inspire some addition, or maybe revision, but nope. Our car broke down, and we took a Lyft to some sad, damp cranny of the Gulf. We got the kind of sunburn that looks like a bruise. A bully of a beach dog kept stealing my son's football.

My grandfather died in the Atlantic Ocean. A former Navy man on vacation with his family, his heart attacked while he was on a raft relaxing. My uncles swam out to save him. The ambulance pulled way down onto the sand. My mother has had skin cancer. Needles wash up on the New Jersey shores. Sand gets in your underwear. See where my feelings about the beach come from? No big loss to be five hours from the coast now.

Ever since I had a seizure, music doesn't sound the same to me anymore. I can no longer stand the sound of guitars, or even the human singing voice. This, of course, is most music. What's replaced it is an interest in the fringes of music, you might say "music," something between the sound of rhythmic car crashes and the whir of a running dishwasher. I do miss regular music in the sense that you could enjoy it with other people. Sing along. But my family mocks my new tastes and my friends save the mix I made for them for another time. When I listen to one of these "songs" online, I'm like the fortieth person to ever even hear it.

I haven't asked Grace what it looked like when I had the seizure. I'm scared to do it. I'm not sure if my son saw me either. I do remember that I had just put up the Christmas tree and lay down on the couch because I didn't feel well. The next thing I remember is a gruff paramedic demanding to know who the president was. I was rolling out the front door. I remember thinking it was a stupid question but could barely respond. Next, I remember some kind of test, a machine, I guess an MRI. I made a joke to myself about that scene in *The Exorcist* where the possessed Regan is being scanned for problems, maybe proof that my brain was already running on some backup programming. My son sometimes does this dance that he calls the "seizure dance," which makes me feel funny, but, again, I don't think he's being cruel.

A good friend of mine died from brain cancer and I did not go to his funeral because I (a) couldn't afford a plane ticket, and (b) was afraid of flying. I am still broke, but I've gotten better about airplanes, as it has been years since I've had a bad flight. Once, flying from Las Vegas to Philadelphia, the bottom dropped out over Texas, and my drink slammed against the ceiling of the airplane. I mean, people screamed. But of course, air travel is the safest blah, blah, blah, despite 525 mph, despite 37,000 feet, despite being trapped in a tube with strangers, despite breathing artificial air. I tried the Greyhound and Amtrak for a while, but these options were like slow death. Better to go in some exhilarating and spectacular way. Not like cancer.

I dream about that friend with some regularity, but the dreams are mainly neutral. No shock that he is alive, or wisdom from beyond the grave. Just some small grief when I wake up. Still, I have other living friends that I dream about less, so maybe there is something to it. I heard a woman on the radio say that she doesn't fear death because historically speaking, as in the history of the human race, just about everyone has already walked through that door. It's the living who are rare and lonely.

I hope one of the takeaways from this letter is not that I'm the type of person who sits around thinking about death all the time. With the help of a few pills, I'm relatively happy and healthy. I coach my son's soccer team and tutor student athletes at the university. Imagine that, me, an ex punk skateboarder, in that kingdom of jocks! They like my tattoos and I like their vitality and positivity. They grieve for nothing, even when they have to wait at the elevator bank because they are on crutches. Due to NCAA regulations, I can't say a lot more. I'm also not allowed to place bets on college sports or wear any other team's gear either.

I live in Mississippi, which is more than just hot and racist. There are turkey vultures, and frogs at night. So many dogs, all half pit bulls. It's also very green. For instance, the sky turned green one morning when I was taking my son to daycare. The rain was coming down so hard I could barely see out of the windshield. The radio cut out; my son, a blabbermouth, went silent.

The advice for tornados was to get out of your car and lay in a ditch as it passes. Safe in my brick house, this advice would always bring a snort. But now, there it was, the moment of truth. Would I pull over on the highway, get my toddler out of the car, and lay on top of him in some muddy trench? Was it more or less cowardly than to keep driving? Why was embarrassment figuring into my decision? I mean, my son and I survived, though when the storm went through to Smithville, some didn't. During my indecision, I saw three state troopers pulled over in a parking lot, and I decided to pull in next to them instead. Imagine that, me, an ex punk skateboarder, glad to see the cops! They offered no advice or encouragement, nor did they lie in a ditch. The sky turned back to gray, the cops pulled out, and my son started talking again. Off to daycare.

Since I began this letter, two more of my bettas have died (leaving two survivors, hearty bros). It occurs to me now that the problem might be the water. The same water we drink, and bathe in, and cook with. Maybe the bettas are swimmy canaries. But I won't call a plumber because my fish have died. I'm stubborn and embarrassed in this way, a difficult mixture. Will I get more fish or just mourn, move on and dismiss the original dream that held such absurd promise? The type of person I am, instead of diligently testing the water I *pour* for *my* family, I'm thinking of a nicer aquarium for newer fish, one with a filter and a light and legitimate room to swim.

Here's a better picture of me if you're thinking of writing back. I once thought for sure I saw a UFO, a whole fleet of them actually, triangles of lights moving across the night sky without a sound. I did not take a picture, but I turned to my Grace and said knowingly, "The Black Triangle. I've finally seen it." My heart was pounding, and an amazing feeling of validation swept through my body—all those science fiction novels I'd read, the grainy YouTube videos, Ancient fucking Aliens, and now me! Imagine that, me, an ex punk skateboarder witnessing the profound. Imagine my disappointment—the grief—I felt when I learned the next morning that a local charity for breast cancer had released dozens of balloons with little candles inside them as a show of solidarity and awareness-making for their cause. I had not seen a UFO, but grief lit up and rising.

Best,

Acknowledgements

Claire and Liam. Zeke and Luna. Mom and Dad. Bill and John. The Mischkers and the Gigueres. Rick Mitchell and Neal Walsh and Will Gorham.

Alan Good, Zach Kocanda and Malarkey Books. Josh Dale and Thirty West. All the editors who published these stories previously. Renee Zuckerbrot. Catherine Lacy and the Tin House Summer Workshop. Meg Pokrass, Gary Finke, and Deb Olin Unferth from the *Best Microfiction* series.

The students, staff, and board at Base Camp Coding Academy. The students and staff at the FedEx Student Athlete Academic Support Center at UM.

The Mississippi Arts Commission for their continued support. The Yokshop writers. Becca and Zachary at TIN. Dawn and the Woven Series.

Stories in this collection have been previously published in:

Sledgehammer Lit, Punk Noir Magazine, Schuylkill Valley Journal, Passages North, ExPat, Hobart, Rejection Letters, The Adroit Journal, Bending Genres, Twin Pies Literary, Day One, Coven Editions Deathcap, X-R-A-Y, Misery Tourism, Versification, BULL Magazine, Maudlin House, Autofocus, Jellyfish Review, trampset, Lumiere Review, New World Writing, Diagram, HAD, Queen Mob's Tea House, Pithead Chapel, No Contact, Quarter After Eight, (mac)ro(mic), Scissor and Spackle, Tiny Molecules, Abandon Journal, Alien Buddha Zine, Ligeia Magazine, The Disappointed Housewife, Wigleaf, Little Engines, Gastropoda, Flash Frog, Litro Magazine, Babel Tower Notice Board, Bullshit Lit, Emerge Literary Journal, Streetcake Magazine, Many Nice Donkeys, JMWW, The Rumpus

SEAN ENNIS is the author of *Cunning, Baffling, Powerful* (Thirty West) and *Chase Us: Stories* (Little A), and his fiction has recently appeared in *Diagram*, *Pithead Chapel*, *Wigleaf*, and *New World Writing*, among others. He lives in Water Valley, MS, with his family, where he directs a nonprofit school training high school graduates to be software developers. More of his work can be found at seanennis.net.

Other Titles from Malarkey Books

Faith, a novel by Itoro Bassey
The Life of the Party Is Harder to Find Until You're the Last One Around, poems by Adrian Sobol
Music Is Over, a novel by Ben Arzate
Toadstones, stories by Eric Williams
Deliver Thy Pigs, a novel by Joey Hedger
It Came From the Swamp, edited by Joey Poole
Pontoon, an anthology of fiction and poetry
What I Thought of Ain't Funny,
edited by Caroljean Gavin
Guess What's Different, essays by Susan Triemert
White People on Vacation, a novel by Alex Miller
Your Favorite Poet, poems by Leigh Chadwick,
Sophomore Slump, poems by Leigh Chadwick
Man in a Cage, a novel by Patrick Nevins
Fearless, a novel by Benjamin Warner
Don Bronco's (Working Title) Shell, a novel?
by Donald Ryan
Un-ruined, a novel by Roger Vaillancourt
Thunder From a Clear Blue Sky,
a novel by Justin Bryant
Kill Radio, a novel by Lauren Bolger
The Muu-Antiques, a novel by Shome Dasgupta
Backmask, a novel by OF Cieri

Gloria Patri, a novel by Austin Ross
Where the Pavement Turns to Sand,
stories by Sheldon Birnie
Still Alive, a novel by LJ Pemberton
I Blame Myself But Also You, stories by Spencer Fleury
Sleep Decades, stories by Israel A. Bonilla
Thumbsucker, poems by Kat Giordano
The Great Atlantic Highway & Other Stories,
by Steve Gergley
First Aid for Choking Victims,
stories by Matthew Zanoni Müller

Death of Print Titles

Consumption & Other Vices, a novel by Tyler Dempsey
Awful People, a novel by Scott Mitchel May
Drift, a novel by Craig Rodgers
The Ghost of Mile 43, a novel by Craig Rodgers
One More Number, stories by Craig Rodgers
Francis Top's Grand Design, stories by Craig Rodgers
Francis Top's Lost Cipher, stories by Craig Rodgers

www.ingramcontent.com/pod-product-compliance
Lightning Source LLC
LaVergne TN
LVHW041937070526
838199LV00051BA/2825